RENÉE

Vivian Schurfranz

SCHOLASTIC INC.
New York Toronto London Auckland Sydney

ISBN 0-590-42043-7

12 11 10 9 8 7 6 5 4 3 2 1   9/8 0 1 2 3 4/9

Printed in the U.S.A.   01

First Scholastic printing, January 1989

RENÉE

A *SUNFIRE* Book

SUNFIRE

To
Harry
with love
always
V.

Chapter One

RENÉE Conti painstakingly wrote in her diary, knowing she'd soon be asked to help with supper, and her mother would be annoyed to find her bending over her writing again. Renée's mother said she wasted too much time on writing and reading, filling her head with poetry and history. Mrs. Conti stressed the importance of being educated, but being educated for marriage. Get a high school diploma, get married, and raise a family. That was her parents' plan for her. Smoothing out the diary's page, Renée sighed, unable to change the way she felt about wanting a career. She began to write a little faster, her letters neat and well formed:

December 20, 1887

Dear Diary,

Today at the bike shop I sold a two-wheeler to a handsome young man who paid the $300 price without even taking a breath. Then he shocked me by asking me to go out with him. Naturally, I refused, but I have a feeling Mr. Steven Morison will be back.

Poor Tony didn't feel well today and had to stay home from school. Father was upset that Tony had to miss a day. He says a son needs to be educated. Oh, like Mother, he wants me educated, too, but in a different way. I want to learn about literature and history and geography, not just cooking and sewing. My parents want me to graduate from high school, but then I'm expected to marry. But no matter what they say, I intend to be a newspaper-woman!

I wonder what they'd say if they knew I wanted to go on to The University of the City of New York and take courses. I can hear Father now. College? No. You marry. Raise a family!

Sometimes I wish I could trade places with eleven-year-old Tony, who'll be encouraged to go on with his schooling. But I don't begrudge my little brother his future. One of these days he'll not only be well educated but also popular with girls. With those even white teeth and *soulful brown eyes, Tony can even soften Father in the middle of a scolding.*

"Renée!" her mother said, standing in the doorway, one hand on her hip. "Didn't you hear me call you?" she asked, an exasperated look on her strikingly handsome face.

"No, Mother, sorry," Renée said, scrambling off the bed and closing her diary.

"Watch the spaghetti sauce and set the table," her mother said, surveying her. She paused and her blue eyes narrowed. "You're growing up, Renée," she commented.

Renée smiled, giving her a hug. "I'm fifteen, Mother," she teased. "And on January the first I'll be sixteen."

"Sixteen," her mother murmured, her face softening. "I remember when we wheeled you in a baby carriage through Central Park. Where does the time go?" She brushed back a few strands of black hair that had fallen across her forehead. "Hurry, Renée. We have two hungry men to feed."

"Three, with Tony," corrected Renée.

"Tony won't be eating tonight," she said, walking ahead to the kitchen. "He still doesn't feel well. But you can be sure your father and Frank will make up for him. Frank, especially. Your older brother could eat a horse!"

"I thought Frank was on the night shift," Renée replied.

"No," Mrs. Conti answered, sprinkling the Italian plums with sugar. "He's only a rookie cop, but yesterday he was transferred to days."

"I'm glad," Renée said as she lifted the lid from the saucepan, humming a tune. A little smile played across her lips. Even though her mother was French, she cooked Italian food to please her husband. She remembered what Olga Zaijeck, her classmate, had said about her own parents. Even though Olga's mother came from Norway, she learned to bake poppy-seed kolaches, roast a goose, and make sauerkraut for her Bohemian husband. I guess that is what a good housewife does, Renée thought, as she swept aside the curtain covering the cupboard and took down five plates. You catered to your husband and put his needs above your own. Going into the dining room, she straightened the checked tablecloth on the round dining-room table and wondered if it had always been like this through the ages.

Aunt Olivia, her father's older sister, emerged from the bedroom, and Renée gave her a quick smile. Olivia, tall and thin, was only five years older than Mr. Conti, but she looked at least ten years older. Renée loved her aunt and was glad she lived with them. "Have you finished, Aunt Olivia?" she asked.

"Finished?" A small smile twisted one corner of her aunt's lean face. "I'll never be finished with the orders for lace collars from Mr. Minsk. His sewing

4

ladies must make fifty dresses a day. When I give him five collars, he wants ten. When I give him ten, he wants twenty, and when I hand him twenty, he wants forty." She shrugged, her eyes warming when she gazed at Renée. "Well, so it goes, and I'm glad for the work. I have one more collar to do before supper. That will make ten today."

Renée quickly calculated that at fifteen cents a collar, Olivia made only $1.50 today. There was no doubt, however, that Olivia was a worker. She wanted to contribute to the household so she wouldn't be a burden. But the Contis didn't need her money. I guess, Renée thought, we're a middle-class family. Her father made a good living from the Wheel and Bike Shop, which he owned, and where she worked part-time.

"And how many bicycles did you sell today?" Olivia asked, arranging a napkin at each place.

"I sold two Safeties," Renée answered, reaching for the carafe of wine mixed with water on the buffet. Setting the decanter on the table, she went on. "Father was very pleased."

Aunt Olivia stopped, one red-checked napkin hanging limply in her hand. Finally she said crisply, her face darkening, "Don't get any ideas about working full-time, Renée. You must finish high school." She shook a finger under her niece's nose. "I want you to be the first girl in the Conti family to graduate from high school."

Renée smiled at her aunt, happy that she was

always so concerned about her. "I'm going to finish, Aunt Olivia, don't worry." She giggled. "Father would skin me alive if I didn't. But I haven't brought up working on a newspaper." And although she still smiled, every time she thought of telling him her plans, her pulse picked up a beat.

"We'll find a way," Olivia said, lovingly patting Renée's cheek. Her dark dress and dark hair made her look stern, but Renée knew that beneath that harsh exterior was a warm, loving heart.

Placing the wooden-handled forks and knives by each plate, Olivia said in a voice of remembrance, "In Italy I married at sixteen, and when Rinaldo died twenty years ago, I had no one to turn to except your father, in America."

"I'm glad he sent you a steamship ticket to come and live in New York," Renée said.

"Yes," Aunt Olivia said, "John has been a good brother." She rested her hands on a high-backed chair. "But if I'd had a skill, I could have stayed in Rome and lived in my own house." She turned toward the bedroom she shared with Renée. "As it is, I feel I don't contribute enough."

"Don't ever think such a thing," Renée said firmly. "You've given us a lot."

"Oh," Olivia said, shrugging her bony shoulders, "perhaps I do earn enough to buy my food and give something toward the household expenses."

"Not to mention your love and caring," Renée said warmly. "Sometimes I think you understand me better than my own mother does."

"Josephine loves you and has reared a fine family. She only wants the best for you and believes a good marriage is the way for a girl to have a secure future."

"Like marriage to Nick DiLeo, for example?" Renée asked dryly.

"Nick's a sweet boy, and he's the son of Sam DiLeo. Josephine knows Nick will inherit a very profitable bakery business. You couldn't find a better man than Nick."

Renée wrinkled her small nose. "Nick and I grew up together. He's like my brother."

Olivia moved closer, lifting Renée's long hair over her collar. She hesitated, crossing her arms and gazing at her niece. "I shouldn't give you advice contrary to Josephine's."

"Please," coaxed Renée, "go on."

"I just want you to taste a little of life first. Don't marry with the idea it will mean security. Look at me. Whoever thought Rinaldo would die at forty-five?" She crossed to the doorway, turning. "I wasn't prepared to support myself." She gave a sour chuckle. "Oh, yes, I could scrub and clean and make pasta, but I couldn't make a decent living."

Renée didn't know what to say. She only gazed at her aunt, remembering the 1847 wedding portrait on the dresser. Forty years ago! Rinaldo and Olivia stood stiffly side by side, staring solemnly at the artist. Olivia's large dark eyes dominated her small young face, and a semblance of a smile hovered about her full lips. She wasn't pretty, but there was an arresting quality about her. The sixteen-year-old girl stood next to her bridegroom, who was a big rawboned Italian man with a black handlebar mustache and long sideburns. The wedding couple looked more bewildered than happy.

"I'll finish the collar before supper," Olivia said, her back straight and not a hair out of place in the braids coiled around her head, as she went inside and closed the door.

"Renée," Mrs. Conti called, "the sauce is bubbling. Are you watching it? I have to put the bread in the oven."

"Be right there," Renée answered, but she moved slowly, thinking of her aunt's advice. She wouldn't marry young, she promised herself, and after graduation she'd take courses at the university and work on a newspaper, no matter what! Walking into the cozy kitchen, she pushed back the starched white curtains and looked out at the darkening sky. Snow patches covered the ground and coated the maple's branches. She loved winter. Especially at Christmastime!

Stirring the red spaghetti sauce, Renée closed her eyes, letting the spicy aroma fill her nostrils. She couldn't get Aunt Olivia out of her mind. Twenty years before, when Rinaldo had died, Olivia had come to New York to live with her brother. Frank was only a baby then, and she, Renée, hadn't even been born yet. Renée's mother often mentioned how Olivia had helped with the baby, the cooking, and the apartment. There wasn't a time when Renée hadn't known Olivia's sweet presence. She felt so close to her.

Using the ladle, Renée tasted the sauce and nodded in approval, both at the flavor and at Olivia's advice. How Olivia, who wanted to be self-sufficient and who was so bright, must have yearned for a career in years past. Renée suspected her aunt lived some of her lost dreams through her. She wished Olivia could have a life of her own and not be dependent on others. But she was too old to start a new life. Well, at least she had a good home and was loved. And someday, Renée thought determinedly, she'd make Olivia proud of her.

Chapter Two

AFTER supper Renée sat stroking Blackie, her long-haired cat, while reading her English assignment, "The Black Cat," by Edgar Allan Poe. How appropriate, she thought, giving Blackie a hug. She liked all of Poe's writing, but "Annabel Lee," one of his poems, was her favorite.

She glanced up when Frank dropped a shoe he'd finished polishing. Tony, lying on his stomach before the potbellied stove, was adding a column of figures, and her father was reading the newspaper. She could hear Aunt Olivia and Mother chatting in the kitchen while they finished the dishes. She'd offered to help but was told her studies came first. She snuggled deeper in the cushions of the armchair.

On a cold winter night it was cozy to be at home with her family around her.

It was almost 1888, a new year, she thought, gazing at the Christmas tree that was bright with strings of red berries and white popcorn. On January first she'd be sixteen, and in June she'd graduate. She gave her father a sideways glance, studying his strong face ringed with a black beard. What would he say when she told him she wanted to pursue a career after high school? She hadn't realized she'd squeezed Blackie so tightly until he meowed angrily, leaping off her lap. With a sigh she returned to her studies.

Mr. Conti folded his newspaper and said, "Frank, you should have seen your little sister today. Renée sold two Safety bikes!"

"Two?" Frank's dark brows shot upward, and he grinned at her. "You're doing all right, Renée. Don't those bikes cost about $300?"

"Right," she answered proudly. "I sold one to a Miss Sally Pincham, who said she needed it to get around to her suffragist meetings, and another to Steven Morison." She said the name casually, but the image of the young man with a head of wavy blond hair came back to her. His pleasant manner and smiling attention had flustered her. He'd asked so many questions, some that she thought were a little obvious, and wondered later if he'd just wanted to keep talking to her.

"Morison?" Frank muttered, smoothing his thick

black mustache. "Does he belong to the Morison family who owns the New York *Gazette*?"

Her pulse quickened. Did he? "I don't know," she said, thinking how well dressed he'd been in his natty plaid suit and how impeccably tailored his belted jacket and creased trousers had looked.

"Was it Morison with one 'r'?" Frank asked.

"Yes, I wrote his name on the sales slip."

"They're the Morisons who own the New York *Gazette*."

"They are?" she asked. To think, Steven Morison's family owned the *Gazette*!

"Well, Renée, sell a few more bikes, and we'll move over to Fifth Avenue, where the Morisons live." Frank threw back his head, laughing.

John Conti smiled, shaking his head. "Our apartment is comfortable. No matter how good business is, we'll stay on Seventy-fourth Street!"

Renée smiled at her father. "It's the best apartment in New York." And it was, too, she thought. They had a three-bedroom flat with large rooms, a modern kitchen with an icebox and a stove with gas burners, and lots of windows covered with ruffled white muslin curtains that let the light filter through. Her mother had tastefully furnished each room, using the latest ideas from the *Ladies Home Journal*. She glanced about at the furniture with colorful blue-and-red cushions, the patterned rug, and the heavy brass gas-jet chandelier. Yes, she liked it here.

Olivia came in, wiping her hands on her apron, followed by Mrs. Conti with a large bowl of fruit. Mr. Conti, after taking a bunch of grapes, moved to the rolltop desk in the corner to check accounts.

Reaching for an apple, Renée secretly hoped Steven Morison would return to the shop.

And to her surprise, he did return — the very next day.

"Hello, Renée," he said, taking off his derby and running his fingers through his thick hair to smooth it down. "I've come back for another bike," he said with a smile.

Her eyes widened as she watched him take off his fur-collared coat, and with his hands behind his back, stroll about the shop, scrutinizing first one bicycle, then another. He stopped to examine the high wheel, or Ordinary, running his slim fingers over the front wooden-spoked wheel that was taller than he was. "Not this one," he said grinning. "Although they do say yapping dogs can't touch you from this altitude. This is a Christmas present for my sister, Megan. If she fell from this height, she'd break her neck." He pointed to a tricycle. "Maybe a three-wheeler would be safer." He mused, turning and looking quizzically at Renée. "What would you suggest?" But before she could reply, he moved to an old Velocipede in the corner. "How about this?" he asked, pulling on the bell.

"No, no," she laughed. "Not a bone-shaker. Those

heavy bikes are out of date." She picked up a card
near the cumbersome machine and read liltingly:

> " 'It never runs away
> And it doesn't take much to feed;
> It's thoroughly reliable —
> The new Velocipede.
> Upon the way you work your legs
> And feet depends its speed;
> And that's about the total of
> The new Velocipede.' "

She held up the card showing the picture of a girl
biker wearing bloomers.

"Is that the latest for bike riding?" Steven asked.

"Not for men," Renée teased. "Here." She
reached for a second card and handed it to him.
"This is what the well-dressed gentleman would
wear."

He took the list and read aloud:

> " 'Jacket
> knickerbockers or breeches
> waistcoat
> shirt
> gaiters
> soft knockabout helmet
> white straw hats, rough or smooth, with ribbon
> cap covers
> stockings

gloves

silk handkerchiefs or mufflers in club colors.'

"I'll have to stock up," Steven said, chuckling. "Now, about Megan's bike. What should I buy?"

"Well," Renée said, moving to the center of the shop and pointing to the ceiling where a shiny nickel-plated bicycle dangled from attached wires. "The Safety is the newest bicycle, and I think the best. It's light and fast and happens to be the one you bought the other day, Mr. Morison. I think your sister would love it."

"Is that what you ride?"

She laughed. "I do, but not in this snow and ice. I've been taking the trolley to work."

"How far do you live from here?"

She hesitated. Did she dare tell him where she lived? Then looking at his pleasant, open face, she saw no harm. "On East Seventy-fourth Street."

"Near Central Park?"

"Yes, not too far."

"It would be fun riding one of these through the park," he said, touching a tandem two-seater and giving her a sideways glance.

She felt her face grow hot. My cheeks must be as red as the ribbon at my throat, she thought.

"But spring's too long to wait." He chuckled. "Would you go ice-skating with me next week?" he asked suddenly.

"Yes, I'd like to," she said, surprising herself at how quickly she answered.

"I'll be in the day after New Year's with my skates," he said, a sparkle in his green eyes. "Is that all right with you?"

She nodded numbly. "That will be fine," she said in a low voice. Hastily, she moved to a blue Safety bicycle on the floor. "Do you still want to purchase a Safety bike?" she asked in her most businesslike voice.

"Of course," he said, reaching into his rear pocket for his wallet. "Just don't forget our date on January second."

The next few days were a flurry of Christmas festivities — going to mass at St. Joseph's, baking pies and cakes, decorating cookies, and singing carols around the fir tree, which was lit with a hundred candles.

On New Year's Day, Mr. and Mrs. DiLeo, their son, Nick, and seven-year-old daughter, Laura, were invited to celebrate the New Year and Renée's sixteenth birthday. Nick and his sister sat on either side of Renée while they finished their roast turkey dinner.

While everyone talked and laughed, Nick turned to Renée and said in a light voice, "You must be thinking pleasant thoughts."

She started guiltily, dabbing at her mouth with her napkin. If Nick knew she was dreaming of going ice-skating with Steven tomorrow, he'd be very un-happy. "Oh," she said casually, "I was thinking that it's 1888, and it's wonderful being here with everyone."

Nick gazed at her for a moment, then lifted his glass and said, "Happy birthday, Renée. You're six-teen, and I hope 1888 brings you happiness, and," a grin lighted up his face, "love."

She smiled impishly. "To love," she said, raising her glass, clinking it against his.

"Here, here," Mr. Conti boomed, a broad smile on his face. "What's going on down at that end of the table? Our two young people are drinking a toast without including us." He lifted his dark brows and stroked his beard, leaning across the table and smirking at Mr. DiLeo. "What do you think of that, Sam?"

Mr. Samuel DiLeo, a small man with brown hair that was mixed with a few gray strands, laughed. "It must be love, eh, John?" He turned to his wife. "What do you say, Momma?"

Ida DiLeo nodded knowingly and smiled at Re-née. "Never mind, Sam. Let the young people alone."

Tony groaned. "Mushy stuff," he muttered.

Frank gave Tony's ear a good-natured tweak. "You'll find out one of these days."

Seven-year-old Laura giggled, and soon the whole table rocked with laughter.

Renée, hearing Mr. DiLeo and her father mention

"wedding," as they continued their conversation, blushed, pushing aside her mincemeat pie. It was embarrassing that every time she was with Nick she was teased. She saw her father wink at Mr. DiLeo. She'd always enjoyed being with Nick, but lately she felt uncomfortable. It was as if they were two dolls and her father wound them up, maneuvering them into each other's arms.

When the men went into the parlor, Renée helped Olivia clear the table while Josephine and Ida DiLeo did the dishes.

After the DiLeos left, Renée sat at the dining room table with Aunt Olivia. "I wish Father and Mr. DiLeo would quit looking at me as if I were dressed in a wedding gown," Renée said.

Olivia, using the candlesnuffer, doused the six tapers. "Your father will come around," she said positively. "He just wants to see his little girl happy."

"Well, I'd be much happier if I were encouraged to work before marriage." Renée paused. "I didn't want to tell him that I'm seeing Steven Morison tomorrow."

Olivia laughed. "Maybe you should tell him while he's in such a good mood. After all, it *is* your birthday."

But Renée didn't get the chance. After everyone had left, she went into the kitchen to pour a glass of milk, and when she came out, her father had already gone to bed. She wondered what he'd say when he found out she'd gone out with someone other than Nick. Well, she couldn't worry about that.

As she undressed and stood in her camisole before the mirror, she thought, I'm sixteen and I'm growing up. Her body had developed curves, and although her waist was tiny and her hips too slim, her formerly round cheeks had disappeared, leaving instead two fine hollows and delicate high cheekbones. Even her lashes seemed longer, shadowing her azure-blue eyes. She undid her long black hair, letting the rich waves fall over her creamy shoulders and onto her white lacy top.

Slipping into bed, Renée lay staring into the darkness for a long time, wondering what the future would bring. She heard her aunt come in and get into the other twin bed. Renée felt comforted knowing Aunt Olivia was there.

Chapter
Three

THE next afternoon, promptly at two o'clock, Steven arrived. Renée greeted him at the door, and when he saw her, he gave a low whistle. He made her feel so pretty in her new outfit that she almost twirled around. The red-and-green plaid skirt flared around her high-topped shoes, and her snug-fitting green jacket had a white fur collar with a matching muff. Atop her thick, long hair she wore a perky hat with a red feather.

"You look terrific," Steven exclaimed, appraising her with obvious approval.

"Why, thank you," she replied, her blue eyes twinkling.

"Shall we go?" He held out his arm for her to take.

"First I want you to meet my mother and my aunt."

"Good," he said, following her into the parlor.

After introductions were made, he settled himself in the horsehide chair and graciously chatted with them. Renée learned he had come home from Harvard University after his father's death to settle the estate and help his mother manage the *Gazette.*

When they left, Renée stepped up into the two-seated carriage while Steven expertly took the reins. She leaned against the plush cushions, happy to be beside him.

Arriving in Central Park, they strapped on their ice skates and glided out onto the rink.

Crossing hands in front, Steven and Renée skimmed over the ice, in and out of the crowds of skaters. On such a sunny January day, it seemed as if every New Yorker was trying out new skates.

"You're graceful," Steven said, smiling at her.

"I'm a better cyclist," she said, "but I love to skate. And," she added, "you're not a bad skater yourself, Mr. Morison."

"Steven," he corrected, grinning at her.

"Steven," she repeated, liking his name and liking him.

Suddenly he skated ahead, then turned and skated backward, doing a fancy figure eight on the glassy surface.

Renée clapped her hands. "Bravo, Steven."

He laughed and raced around the rink, stopping

up short before her. His skates cut deeply into the frozen surface, throwing off shavings of ice. Breathless, he looked down at her. "You know," he said with a broad smile, "the cold has turned your cheeks rosy, and your eyes sparkle like blue crystals."

Renée glanced away, embarrassed at his open admiration. All at once she felt flustered, and she skated to a nearby bench, not knowing how to reply.

Laughing, he pulled her back onto the ice.

After skating for over two hours, he grabbed her hand and drew her toward him. "Time for hot chocolate. I know just the place."

Seated beside him in his carriage, she felt like a princess driving down Fifth Avenue, behind two prancing chestnuts. They rode past the Metropolitan Museum of Art and elegant town houses, until they came to a small cafe called The Bluebird.

Inside, gilt-framed mirrors lined the walls, reflecting charming chairs with heart-shaped backs. Steven led her to a corner table for two.

Sipping her hot chocolate, Renée relaxed, feeling warm and glowing after such an exhilarating afternoon. The skating was fun, and Steven was delightful. "Do you miss Harvard?" she asked, studying his strong, yet gentle face.

"Yes," he replied, with a slight shrug of his shoulders, "but I'll go back to Boston in a few months. Then, after I finish college, I'll work on the paper. If Mother wants to keep on as publisher of the *Ga-*

zette, I'll be her assistant, but if she's ready to retire, I'll take over."

"You'll run the *Gazette*?" she whispered in disbelief. "How wonderful."

"Are you interested in newspaper work?" he asked, his head tilting to one side and lines of amusement crinkling about his eyes.

"Very much," she replied, hesitating. Did she dare tell him how much she wanted to be a newspaperwoman? She didn't want him to feel obligated to her. When she got a job on a newspaper, she wanted to do it on her own. But finally she blurted out, "I'm going to be a journalist someday."

"A journalist?" He gave her a questioning look. "There aren't any female journalists."

"Are you forgetting your mother is the head of one of the most powerful papers in New York?"

"That's different," he said. "I meant there aren't any women roving reporters."

"There happen to be almost six hundred women reporters," she said, a suggestion of annoyance hovering in her eyes.

"Really?" he said, the glint of amusement returning.

"And there are well-known newspaperwomen," she went on, her voice ringing. "What about Jennie June at the New York *Herald*?" She paused, glaring at him. "And Sally Joy, who became 'Penelope Penfeather' of the Boston *Herald* and who also became the first president of the New England Women's Press Association."

"My, my, I had no idea," he said softly, trying to suppress a smile.

"And there's Fanny Fern at the Philadelphia *Ledger* and Grace Greenwood at the New York *Times* and Nelly Bly at the *Herald*, and — "

"Whoa." He held up his hands, chuckling. "You've done your research, that's for sure."

"I've read a lot about newspapers and women journalists," she said with a smile. "I hope you'll forgive me if I sounded too excited about the subject."

"You're forgiven." He reached over, his fingertips touching hers. For an instant she allowed his hand to linger close to hers, then she gently withdrew it.

"You know, I'll bet you'll make a great reporter."

"I know I will," she said confidently. But she didn't tell Steven about her father's plans for her or anything about her friend Nick. Father! she suddenly thought. "What time is it?" she asked in a panic.

Steven pulled out the chain dangling from his vest pocket and flipped open the cover of his gold watch. "Exactly seven o'clock."

"Oh, no," she said in dismay, hastily gathering her gloves, muff, and skates. "I've missed supper. I must go." She jumped to her feet while Steven paid the check.

After arriving at the Contis' brownstone apartment house, Renée waved good-night to Steven as she ran up the front steps.

"When will I see you again?" he asked, his hat in hand and his bright gold hair blowing in the wind.

"I don't know," she said, "but I must go in. Father will be upset that I missed supper. He's a stickler for punctuality."

"Then I'll come in the bike shop later this week," Steven called. But she didn't reply as she quietly opened the door and slipped inside.

Mr. and Mrs. Conti and Aunt Olivia were in the parlor, and Renée hurriedly put her skates away, hung up her jacket, and placed her hat on the shelf.

"Hi, everyone," she said cheerfully, coming into the room.

John Conti slowly put down his newspaper. "You missed supper, Renée," he stated, his face darker than usual.

"I-I know. We were talking and the time flew." She gave him a small smile, hoping there wouldn't be a scene, but from his next words she knew she was going to have trouble.

"Who is this Steven Morison whom your mother mentioned?" Her father's voice was soft.

"He's the fellow that bought the two Safety bicycles," Renée replied.

"It's Nick DiLeo you should be out with," her father said, glowering at her. "Nick would have gotten you home in time for supper."

"I'm sorry," Renée said meekly, focusing on her

father's hands. She knew he was annoyed by the way his fingers drummed on the chair arms. What dextrous hands, she thought, hands that could fix anything. In the back of the shop he repaired broken handlebars, wheels, or pigskin seats. He understood everything about bicycles. Her eyes shifted to his craggy face, wishing he could understand her.

"So this Steven Morison owns the *Gazette*?" Her father's piercing brown eyes bore into hers.

"His mother does," she answered, a glimmer of hope surfacing. Perhaps she could reason with him after all. "He goes to Harvard," she explained.

"A big shot, eh? Well, you're not to see him anymore!"

She stared at him, stupefied. "Why not?" she asked, defiantly. "Steven Morison's a perfect gentleman."

"You're not to see him again," her father repeated, emphasizing each word. "You're promised to someone else."

Renée felt as if a bucket of ice water had spilled down her spine. "Promised?" she whispered.

Her father squirmed uneasily. "I wasn't ready to discuss this yet, but you might as well know. Sam DiLeo and I had a long talk today, and we discussed a wedding alliance. You and Nick."

Renée dug her nails into her palms, but she didn't dare answer her father back. Not when he was this upset.

"Your wedding will take place in one year, when you'll be seventeen." He softened a little, saying gently, "You'll be ready to marry, Renée, you'll see. Marriage is good, isn't it, Josephine?"

Renée's mother put down her darning. "It is good." Love shone from her dark eyes when she looked at John Conti.

"But I don't love Nick," Renée protested, flinging out her hands helplessly. "Don't I have anything to say? Doesn't Nick have anything to say? Maybe he doesn't want to marry me, either."

"Nick loves you. He wants to marry you. Just think, one day he'll own his father's bakery."

Mrs. Conti nodded knowingly, putting her knitting aside. "You'll be secure, Renée."

Tears stung Renée's eyes. "I can take care of myself! I want to work for a living!"

"Did you hear that, Josephine? Renée wants to work! That's the most preposterous thing I've ever heard." Mr. Conti's face reddened.

"I can support myself," Renée said. "I intend to get a job on a newspaper." She hadn't meant to tell him of her plans now, but the words just came out. She felt her face warm. Why hadn't she waited until he was in a better mood?

Mr. Conti agitatedly pulled on his beard. "Not another word, young lady! Go to bed!"

"But, Father — "

"No more!" he roared. "You are not working at

any newspaper office, and that's final. The marriage alliance is settled." He grabbed his newspaper, ignoring her.

Olivia, who had also been quietly knitting in the corner, looked up, gazing reproachfully at her brother. "Renée only had an afternoon of fun, ice-skating, John."

"Olivia, the discussion is closed," Mr. Conti said coldly, turning his attention back to his daughter. "Young lady, go to bed."

Olivia faced Renée. "I saved you some supper. Come into the kitchen with me."

"No food!" thundered Mr. Conti. "Get to bed, Renée!"

Sadly, Renée turned and moved toward the room she shared with her aunt. As she went by her mother, Mrs. Conti took her hand, squeezing it.

Renée didn't respond. Why hadn't her mother defended her as Aunt Olivia had? Her mother agreed with her father. Tears blurred Renée's eyes as she opened her bedroom door and closed it.

Leaning against the door, she covered her face with trembling hands, anguish in her heart. Was this the end of her dream?

Chapter Four

WHEN Renée awakened, the house was still. She had only a few more days of vacation, and her father had told her, since business was slow, not to come into the shop. She should enjoy herself instead. But remembering the confrontation of the night before, she wondered how she could ever enjoy herself again. A leaden feeling stole over her body.

Thrusting her arms into her floral wrapper, she went into the kitchen, where her mother and aunt were drinking coffee.

"Good morning, darling," her mother said, smiling.

Renée bent over and kissed her mother's forehead. "Good morning, Mother," she murmured. She kissed Aunt Olivia, then poured herself a cup of coffee.

"I have a surprise for you," Mrs. Conti said. "For a belated birthday gift, your father is giving you a bicycle dress. We'll go to Lord & Taylor and pick one out. Then we'll have lunch at Stewart's. Would you like that?"

Renée's heart leaped. Seldom did they go downtown to the big stores. This would be a real treat. It was so like her father after having an argument to want to patch things up with a gift. He doesn't want me to be angry, she thought, but I can't forget. Nonetheless, she smiled at her mother. "Going shopping will be fun," she said, unable to hide her enthusiasm.

Olivia leaned over. "I'm going to crochet a few collars, then go for an outing. I plan to stop at the bicycle shop and see John. I'll bring him a special lunch and," she winked at Renée, "we'll have a chat. I wouldn't be surprised if I'll have some good news for you when you get home."

"Even if you can't change his mind about the marriage," Mrs. Conti said, picking up her cup and saucer and moving to the sink, "Renée will still have a wonderful future."

"John listens to me," Olivia said thoughtfully. "I just hope I can convince him that Renée's future should be decided by *her*."

"I doubt it," Renée said under her breath, but she gave Olivia a grateful glance.

"John is a fair man," Olivia said. "Don't give up hope. Now go and have a good time with your mother. I'll see you when you get home with a new outfit."

Renée stirred sugar in her coffee, not replying. Aunt Olivia meant well, but her father was stubborn. And her mother really wanted her daughter to marry Nick. A good future, she had said. Good by *her* standards, perhaps, but times were changing.

After dressing, Renée felt her spirits lift. It was a beautiful day, and she liked nothing better than shopping at Stewart's or Lord & Taylor.

Renée went outdoors to wait for her mother, needing fresh air. But when she saw Nick coming up the street, her first inclination was to whirl around and dash back into the house. But, as usual, Nick's face was split into a wide grin and she couldn't be rude to him. It wasn't his fault their fathers were throwing them together.

"And where are you off to?" Nick asked jauntily.

"Shopping," Renée replied, wondering what to say to her husband-to-be. Nick looked down at his feet, still smiling. "I guess you heard about our fathers and the marriage alliance." He gave her a sidelong glance, his eyes twinkling.

"I heard," she said, turning her face away.

Nick took her hand. "You're the only one for me, Renée. You always will be." Suddenly his brow furrowed. "But you look unhappy." His voice caught.

She gazed at him wistfully. Dear Nick. He truly loved her. How could she break his heart and not pretend happiness? They'd been friends too long, shared too many secrets. How could she ever forget the day Nick's dog had died? She and Nick had cried in each other's arms.

"Nick . . . " Renée began in a wavering voice. Tears welled up in her eyes.

"It is the marriage, isn't it?" he asked grimly.

"It's — it's . . . " But words failed her.

"I'll never hold you to an agreement made by our fathers." His hand tightened on hers.

"You don't know Father," she said, hating to see the hurt in Nick's eyes. "It's just that I want time before I marry. And," she added softly, "I'm not sure you're the one for me."

Mrs. Conti came out, slipping on her gloves. "Hello, Nick," she called.

"Hello, Mrs. Conti," Nick answered, his gaze shifting back to Renée. "We'll talk later," he said quietly, releasing her hand.

"Hurry, Renée," her mother said, walking toward the horsecar stop.

"Yes, Mother," Renée said. "Yes, we'll talk later, Nick." Their eyes met, and the only sound was from the melting icicles dripping onto the pavement. All at once, Renée spun about to catch up to her mother.

As they walked away, she glanced over her shoulder to see Nick standing forlornly on the sidewalk.

Straightening her shoulders, she thought of her future, and it didn't include Nick.

Seated beside her mother on the horse-drawn trolley, Renée put Nick out of her mind. It was a pleasant day, which she wanted to enjoy, and she wanted to please her mother.

No one would suspect they didn't live on Fifth Avenue, Renée thought. Her blue coat with a short cape attached and small-brimmed hat were in the latest fashion. Her mother, wearing a smart violet coat and wide-brimmed hat covered with feathers, gazed imperiously out the window as if she did this every day.

Stepping off the trolley, they walked down Broadway until they reached 20th Street. Renée was entranced by the windows, still decorated for Christmas. The street bustled with elegant horse-drawn carriages and red trolleys. And straight ahead on the corner was Lord & Taylor's store, with its majestic towers.

Entering the elegant store, Renée walked down the aisle, where dress dummies, or mannequins, were clothed in the latest style. Women's suits of fine worsted wool trimmed with braid, and elegant dresses were on display. Renée paused before one dress dummy to examine a chiffon evening gown in bright green.

Going into the elevator, she gave her mother a sidelong glance. She'd only been in an elevator twice, and both times, she stood apprehensively, waiting to see what would happen when it started to ascend. Lord & Taylor was one of the first stores to install an elevator, and they'd never had an accident, but it still didn't keep Renée's heart from pounding. If the rope holding the elevator cage should break, they'd plummet to the basement. When her mother took her arm, Renée patted her hand. "It's all right, Mother," she said, biting her underlip.

When the elevator lurched to the third floor, a gentleman ahead of them said to his companion, "No telling how high buildings will go with an elevator installed."

"High as the sky," the other man said with a chuckle.

The doors opened, and the men stepped back so that Renée and her mother could exit first.

Renée tried on a chic two-piece bicycle dress. The yellow bloomers, striped stockings, and balloon-sleeved blouse were set off by elbow-length orange gloves of the finest kidskin. A jaunty straw sailor hat completed the ensemble.

Mrs. Conti told the clerk to wrap it up.

Over lunch, Renée picked at her salad. She hated returning home to face her father. She glanced at her mother's strong, unlined face with her rich dark hair peeking around her wide-brimmed hat. "How old were you when you were married?" she asked suddenly.

Josephine Conti's blue eyes, paler than Renée's, shone. "Seventeen, and I haven't regretted one day."

"And you met Father on the boat coming to America?"

"Yes, on the *Columbia*. I was only nine. I've told you the story before, but now that you're older you can appreciate it. My parents took a liking to John, who was sixteen at the time, and once we'd gone through immigration at Ellis Island, they kept in touch, having him to dinners and Sunday outings. He became one of the family."

"When did you fall in love with him?"

Mrs. Conti laughed. "When I first saw him at the ship's rail, playing a concertina and singing a lively Italian song." She sighed, and her eyes became dreamy. "He waited for me to grow up. When he was twenty-four and I was seventeen, he proposed. One month later, we were married." She became solemn. "That was 1861, the year the Civil War broke out, and the year John volunteered to fight for the Union. He joined the New York Volunteers, and for four years we were separated. During that time I lived with my parents, but as soon as he returned, we rented a small apartment. John bought a bicycle shop, and shortly after that, Frank was born. Then Olivia came to live with us."

Mrs. Conti reached over and squeezed Renée's hand. "Then you were born." She paused, smiling. "I'd been praying for a baby girl, and I've been blessed that you grew into such a lovely, pleasant, and bright young lady."

"What good is it to be bright if I can't use my brains?" Renée asked seriously.

"Let's not ruin today," her mother said, picking up the dress package and quickly changing the subject. "Wait until your father sees your new bicycle outfit."

Renée's heart sank. But she knew she had to face him sooner or later.

When they returned home, Josephine Conti hurried into the kitchen to put the roast on, and Renée went into the bedroom to change into everyday clothes. First, though, she gazed out the window. The sun had disappeared, and the oak's branches scratched against the pane. The gray day was as gray as her mood. What was she to do? she thought. No one would ever convince her father that he'd made a wrong decision.

"Did you have a good day?" Olivia asked, standing in the doorway, a catlike smile on her face.

"Very nice," Renée answered. "Did you see Father?" Surely her aunt's smile meant good news.

"He's agreed that you can see other boys and that maybe you can work in his shop for a while." She sat down at her worktable, watching Renée's reaction.

Renée stared at her aunt. "I can't believe it!" she

cried elatedly. "How did you get him to change his mind?"

"Well," Olivia said, pleased with herself as she folded several lace collars, "I reminded him of Rinaldo's death and of how I had to come to America to live with him and Josephine. He hadn't realized how much I'd wanted to stay in Rome. Or that I wanted to be independent."

Renée ran to Olivia and clasped her arms around her neck, rocking back and forth. "I'm so happy." She stepped back. "I didn't know you were so persuasive."

Olivia laughed, arranging the collars in a neat pile. "Oh, John listens to his older sister — he always has."

"I can't thank you enough, Aunt Olivia. To think — I have a future!" She hesitated. "I wonder what Sam DiLeo will say."

"Oh, your father can be quite persuasive, too," Olivia said. "He'll talk to Sam and," she glanced at Renée, "Nick. I hope he won't be too disappointed."

"No, Nick's too busy at the bakery, and even though he likes me, he isn't in love. He treats me like a sister. Oh, Auntie, do you know what this means?" She twirled around, her skirts flying. "I can see Steven again! I can work on a newspaper!"

"Your father said you could work in *his* shop. He didn't say anything about a newspaper."

"We'll see," Renée said, hugging herself. Now

that she was out of a forced marriage, she could be persuasive, too.

"A girl getting a job on a newspaper won't be easy," Olivia said.

Renée laughed, and when Blackie padded in, she scooped up the cat into her arms and danced around the room. "I've already talked to Mr. Benson at the *Herald*, and I may be an apprentice there."

"You haven't mentioned this before," Olivia said, her dark brows rising as she studied her niece.

"No, I didn't want to tell anyone until I was certain." She sat on the bed, stroking Blackie. "But Mr. Benson came to our English class three weeks ago and offered to take on two apprentices to work on the newspaper."

"And what makes you think you'll be chosen?" Olivia asked doubtfully.

"I ran after him when class was over and told him how eager I was to be a journalist. I even gave him an extra sample of my writing."

"With your determination and energy, I'm certain Mr. Benson was impressed. That would be an honor. Even your father would be proud to have you picked for the *Herald*. When will you know?"

"When school starts on Monday." She put Blackie down and said confidently, "Once I get on the paper, I *know* they'll give me a job after I graduate."

"I hope so," Olivia said slowly.

But even her aunt's doubtful tone couldn't dampen Renée's radiant happiness.

Chapter
Five

THE next day Renée received a note from Steven inviting her to dinner on Saturday. She wanted to go but knew she needed her father's permission. If he really meant what he'd said to Olivia, that she could see other boys, this would be the test.

That evening before her father returned from work, Renée brushed her hair until it gleamed and put on a fresh white apron. She baked apple dumplings, her father's favorite dessert, put the paper and his slippers by his chair, then waited for him to come home. When the time was right, she'd show him Steven's invitation.

Mr. Conti was in a good mood, having sold two tricycles and a Safety bike. After dinner, and after finishing two helpings of apple dessert, he leaned back contentedly in his chair, pinching Renée's cheek. "Delicious, dear one. And to think you made it all for me." He chuckled and his white teeth, surrounded by his black beard and mustache, shone.

Renée hesitated, then followed him into the parlor, handing him Steven's note.

Mr. Conti unfolded the invitation and mumbled aloud: " 'Dinner at seven . . . Forty-eight Fifth Avenue . . . call for you at six-thirty . . . want you to meet my sister and mother.' "

Mr. Conti glanced speculatively at Renée. "Do you want to go?" he asked, bushy eyebrows rising on his forehead.

"Oh, yes," she replied. "Could I?" She held her breath, waiting for his reply.

He sat heavily in his big chair, smoothing his beard. "Olivia and I had a long talk. I want you to be happy. You may see this Steven Morison, but," he warned, shaking his forefinger at her, "you must be home early. By ten o'clock."

"I promise," Renée said ecstatically, scarcely believing how easily her father had given in. A rush of love warmed her, and she ran to kiss his cheek. "Thank you, Father."

He reached up, patting her hand. "I just don't want you hurt."

She laughed softly. "I won't be hurt. Steven is a fine young man. You'll see."

He nodded wearily. "I'm sure he is, but don't forget Nick."

"I could never forget Nick. We grew up together. He's my friend."

Mr. Conti studied his daughter for an instant, then said brusquely, "Go on, now. Let me read." He motioned her away, but the warmth in his eyes softened his gruffness.

Saturday evening, when Renée rode with Steven up to the front of his gray-stone mansion, her hold tightened on the red rose that Steven had presented to her. She hoped his sister and mother would like her. She was delighted, though, when she remembered her father and Steven laughing together over a political cartoon depicting President Grover Cleveland clutched in the arms of big business. Even her father couldn't resist Steven's charm.

Steven, so self-assured and appealing, took her hand as they went up the marble steps with two reclining lions on either side of the wide entrance.

Entering the vestibule, Renée approached the butler, who took her coat and gloves. Then tilting her chin upward, trying to hide her uneasiness, she took Steven's arm and went into the large living room.

She walked on a thick Oriental rug leading into the salon, and her first impression was one of gloom. Gas wall-lamps flickered over the teak-paneled, dark-looking room. Round tables, draped with satin tablecloths, were cluttered with silver-framed pictures, small statues, and vases. Heavy brown velvet drapes covered the tall windows, and ferns on pedestals stood in every corner.

An older woman, red curls piled high on her head and two red patches of rouge on her thin cheeks, hurried forward to greet Renée. She wore a tight-fitting green dress and held an open fan, which she moved rhythmically back and forth. "So," she said in a clipped, clear voice, "this is Renée Conti. Steven's told us so much about you, my dear."

"And Steven has told me about you," Renée said, inclining her head and smiling.

"Come and sit down, Renée." With a sweep of her long hand, Mrs. Morison indicated a cane chair.

Renée glanced beyond Mrs. Morison's bare shoulder to see a lovely blonde girl eyeing her. Mrs. Morison turned slightly. "And this is Megan, Steven's younger sister."

"Younger by only a year," Megan said petulantly. "I just had my eighteenth birthday." She uncrossed her legs and moved gracefully toward Renée. She had flawless skin and brown eyes fringed with long, thick lashes. "I'm happy to meet you, Renée," she said, her lips curling into a half smile.

Renée almost bobbed a curtsy. She felt as if she were in the presence of royalty. Megan, with her long blonde curls caught up in a jet-beaded clasp and her pink silk gown, looked breathtakingly beautiful, like a princess in a fairy tale. But a haughty princess, Renée thought. The way she looks down her small nose at me would unnerve anyone. But with Steven's hand supporting her elbow, Renée became more self-assured. She smiled at Megan. Then, rather than let Megan's cool glance upset her, Renée gazed about at the richly furnished room. A porcelain cat sat before the green marble fireplace, and on the mantel was a tall statue of Venus. The heavy gilt-framed portraits scattered about the room must be of Steven's ancestors. The cold eyes of a stern-faced woman in one frame reminded Renée of Megan's.

"Come, my dears. Dinner is ready," Mrs. Morison said, snapping shut her fan.

Seated at the long dining table, Renée stared bewilderedly at the array of silver, then glanced at Steven, who reassuringly smiled at her. She could scarcely see Mrs. Morison, who sat at the head of the table, because of the huge silver candelabra. Renée carefully lifted her crystal goblet, sipping water, not hurrying to choose a fork. Instead, she observed Megan's choice, then followed her lead.

She was getting along beautifully until Megan, aware of Renée's doubt, deliberately chose the wrong fork, and after Renée began to eat, Megan replaced hers with the correct one. Renée noticed her trick but didn't switch forks. She tried to ignore Megan's smirk but could feel a warm pink steal over her face as she cut her roast beef. She wanted to make Steven proud of her and to get through this fancy dinner with as few mistakes as possible, but his sister was making it difficult. Why was Megan trying to embarrass her? Was she trying to tell her that she was out of her class and to run back to 74th Street, where she belonged?

"And what do you plan to do after you graduate, Renée?" Mrs. Morison asked politely.

Without a moment's hesitation, Renée replied, "I want to be a journalist." Briefly she told her of the open apprenticeships at the *Herald*.

"Newspaper work is demanding," Zena Morison said, "but it seems you've got enough spunk to tackle it." She nodded at the butler, who began to serve the dessert.

This time Renée watched Steven for the correct knife and fork to use on the poached pear.

"And if you don't get a newspaper job," Mrs. Morison persisted, "what then?"

"Oh, I will," she stated firmly.

"I believe you will, at that," Mrs. Morison said quietly, appearing to smile in the flickering candlelight.

"Gaining experience at the *Herald* will help me obtain a permanent position," Renée went on.

"Would you like to tour the *Gazette*?" Steven asked impulsively. "I'll take you through."

"Oh, I'd love it," she said enthusiastically. "Oh, would you, Steven?"

"Next week," he promised.

"I wish Megan showed such eagerness for the

family newspaper," Zena Morison said dryly.

"Mother!" Megan protested.

"I know, dear," Zena Morison said, gazing fondly at her daughter. "You're too caught up in your June wedding plans."

"Yes," she answered, giving Renée a strange look. "You have your career all planned, don't you?" she asked in mild astonishment.

Renée smiled at her. "Yes, I do. It wasn't easy, but my parents have agreed to let me work after graduation. Father wants me to continue in his bicycle shop, but I have other ideas."

Megan, touching her napkin to her lips, gave Renée a puzzled look. "How old are you?"

"I was sixteen last week," Renée responded, amused at Megan's look of disbelief. She went on to explain. "I've wanted to write all my life." She gave a low, throaty laugh. "I write in my diary every night, and Mrs. Porter, my English teacher, says I have talent." Her eyes sparkled. "But even if I didn't, I'd have to write." She tapped her heart. "Something inside here won't let me quit."

"I admire you, Renée," Zena Morison said crisply, smiling briefly. "I think you'll make a fine reporter someday." She pushed back her chair, indicating that the meal was finished. "We'll adjourn to the drawing room."

Renée glowed at Mrs. Morison's remarks. As the head of a big newspaper, Renée found her praise especially gratifying.

Rising, Renée felt she had managed the evening's dinner quite well. She brought up her hand to sweep back an unruly curl, when all at once her lavender-colored beads snapped. In dismay she watched the crystals bounce and roll across the bare oak floors. They scattered in every direction, flying under chairs and beneath the table. How did it happen?

What a clod, she thought, her face as red as the bouquet of roses on the table. She didn't dare look at Megan's triumphant smile. Instead, she knelt on all fours and instantly bumped heads with Megan. What on earth, she wondered, was Megan doing on her hands and knees, picking up her beads?

"Ouch," Renée muttered ruefully, rubbing her head. Abruptly, she sat back on her haunches.

"You have a hard skull," Megan exclaimed, touching her forehead. She laughed impishly, and Renée's discomfort vanished. She chuckled, and soon both girls were giggling together.

By this time, Steven, Mrs. Morison, and the butler were crawling around, gathering beads. Megan wiped the tears of laughter from her eyes, and Renée thought that perhaps Steven's sister wasn't as bad as she'd first thought.

On Monday Renée's step was light as she hurried to school. That day Mrs. Porter was going to announce the two apprenticeships. The crisp air felt fresh, and Renée thought how well everything was going. The next day after school Steven was giving her a tour of the *Gazette*, and she loved being with him. Even his sister had warmed slightly toward her, asking her to lunch soon. She grinned at the thought, knowing Megan just wanted to scrutinize the girl her brother had brought home to dinner. But that was all right. She welcomed an opportunity to get to know Megan better.

Seated in English class, Renée thought the conjugation of verbs would never end. Finally, however, in the last five minutes of class, Mrs. Porter cleared her throat and asked everyone to put their work away.

Renée quickly smoothed her collar, sat up, and folded her hands. She wore a serene smile but silently chastised herself. She shouldn't be so confident, but she knew she was the only student with a straight-A average, and her essays had been singled out by Mrs. Porter to be read aloud.

A smile flickered over Mrs. Porter's round face, and she pulled her short, plump frame up to its full height. "Today," she said happily, "we have two winners who have been chosen to work at the *Herald*." She paused dramatically. "Mr. Benson has chosen Joshua Greene . . . "

Renée turned and smiled at Joshua, who grinned broadly. Then she gave her attention to Mrs. Porter.

" . . . and the second winner is — Thomas Bennigan."

The class applauded, and the sound of clapping

reverberated dimly in Renée's ears. Stunned, she sat rigidly, her frozen smile gradually receding. She wasn't chosen, she thought, devastated. She was passed over. Why? Her heart thudded against her chest.

When the bell rang shrilly, she sat motionless for a moment, tears burning behind her eyes. Then hastily gathering her books, she raced past Mrs. Porter and down the long corridor.

Bolting out into the cold air, she pushed through the crowds of students spilling out the door, but their images were blurred by her tears. Their laughter filled the air as they hurried across the street, dodging carriages and horses. Renée miserably turned toward home. There was no happiness in her heart — only a dull ache.

Chapter Six

FOR the next few days Renée's daily routine didn't vary. She worked at the bicycle shop after school and helped at home, but she didn't have the usual spring in her step. Olivia had warned her, she thought sourly, but she still couldn't believe she hadn't been chosen for an apprenticeship.

She'd even had a conference with Mrs. Porter. But her teacher had only shaken her head, saying that girls were seldom picked for newspaper work.

That afternoon Steven was meeting her after school and taking her to the *Gazette*. Although the disappointment of the lost apprenticeship still lingered, she was looking forward to the tour.

Stuffing her books in her book bag, she hurried outside to where Steven was waiting.

"Hi. Ready to see where I work?" Steven stood straight and tall before her.

His radiant smile cheered her. She answered eagerly, "Yes, I am," and returned his smile.

As they walked to his office, she told him about losing out at the *Herald*.

"That's too bad," Steven said, his compelling green eyes darkening to a deep jade. "I know how much it meant to you." His gloved hand over hers was comforting.

Arriving at the *Gazette*, Steven first took her to the second floor, where the steam-cylinder presses were whirring and where ink-spattered men in coveralls, billed caps, and leather aprons stopped to stare at her. Stepping through the newsprint that littered the floor, she watched in amazement as the newspapers rolled off the press. She wanted to ask a hundred questions, but the noise of the clanking machines made it impossible.

As they walked through an adjoining room, typesetters bending over their linotype machines scarcely looked up. Renée was pleased to see a number of women at this delicate, tedious task. The next area was the composing room, where men sat at their desks, each with a sheaf of news articles, a long sheet of paper, scissors, and paste pots, which they frequently dipped into.

On the first floor were the reporters, some typing, others scribbling, and a few talking. Renée saw no women here. Suddenly a man dashed past her, going into a glassed-in office. He threw a sheet of paper on a heavyset man's desk and rushed out again.

Steven, taking her arm, entered the office and introduced her. "This is Mr. Webb, the managing editor. How's it going, Mike?"

"Fine, fine, Steven, my boy. Good to see you." The bald man, his vest unbuttoned and a cigar in his mouth, clapped Steven on the back.

"This is Renée Conti, who wants to be a newspaperwoman," Steven said, inclining his blond head toward Renée.

Mr. Webb shook her hand, scarcely looking at her. "Better stick to housework," he muttered and turned back to Steven. "Look at this, Steven. It's my new Remington typewriter. Types twice as fast as my old one and the letters come out as clear as printer's type."

As the two men talked, Renée looked around at Mr. Webb's cluttered desk, his telephone, and a funny-looking machine, which was probably a dictaphone.

She was glad to leave the smoky office. Besides, it was obvious Mr. Webb didn't care for her.

"Mother knows you're here and wants you to stop by," Steven said.

"I'd love to," Renée answered.

Entering a small room with a window, Mrs. Morison was seated at her desk, talking on the phone and motioning for them to be seated.

Finishing her conversation, she replaced the receiver and leaned back in her swivel chair. "How do you like the *Gazette*?" she inquired, her hair appearing to be a flaming orange in the harsh daylight.

"It's wonderful," Renée said, her eyes sparkling. "You're lucky to run such a big paper."

"Yes, it's never dull. Right now," she said, "I've sent Larry Oakes over to the hotel to interview Benjamin Harrison. Harrison has thrown his hat in the ring for 1888 and plans to run for President on the Republican ticket against Cleveland." She focused her piercing gray eyes on Renée. "How did you fare at the *Herald*?"

Renée shook her head. "Two boys were chosen."

"They passed up a good opportunity, don't you think so, Mother?" Steven asked, his handsome face breaking into a smile.

Zena Morison, studying Renée's face, picked up a pencil and tapped it on the desk. "How would you like to be an apprentice on the *Gazette*?"

Renée's eyes widened. She could only nod, not daring to speak.

"You'll start on Monday. I'll tell Mr. Webb you'll be coming in after school, and he'll assign you to where you're needed." She gave a dry chuckle. "I think you're a match for Mike Webb, but," she warned, "it won't be easy."

Steven grinned. "And I'm not here much to give you any help."

Renée's chin jutted out. "I don't expect your help.

If I can't do this on my own, then I'm not cut out for newspaper work."

"You'll do it," Steven said confidently.

"I'll work hard for you, Mrs. Morison," Renée said earnestly. "You won't be sorry you've given me this chance."

"I know I won't," Mrs. Morison said briskly. "Now, you two run along. Mayor Abram Hewitt is due any minute. He's an old friend, and there are some personal things I want to discuss with him about your father, Steven."

Arriving back at her apartment, Renée stood on an upper step, looking down at Steven. "I've had a marvelous day, Steven," she said, feeling warm, despite the cold nipping at her cheeks and nose.

"So have I," he answered, resting his hand on her coat sleeve. "You know, I've never known anyone like you, Renée."

She grinned. "I'm an ordinary New York girl," she teased. "What's different about me?"

"I don't know. Maybe your vitality. Maybe your curiosity. Maybe your pleasantness. And," he bantered, "maybe it's those blue, blue eyes."

"Hmmm, I sound like a nice person."

"Nicest one I've ever met," he said lightly.

His soft gaze made her feel warm inside.

"Renée," he said huskily, his arms encircling her waist and pulling her forward.

Suddenly she heard her name. "Hello, Renée," Nick called, coming up the street.

Guiltily she drew back from Steven. "N-Nick," she stammered. "Come and meet my friend Steven Morison."

"I'd say by the looks of things that you're a very *close* friend, Steven," Nick said dryly, holding out his hand. "I'm Nick DiLeo."

Steven laughed. "Renée and I get along well. Pleased to meet you, Nick."

Nick faced Renée. "I haven't seen you since I heard about your lost apprenticeship." His solemn, dark eyes bore into hers. "I'm sorry, Renée."

She'd never thought of him as short before, but next to Steven he didn't look as tall as she'd thought. Nonetheless, Nick had a quick grace about him.

"Everything has turned out all right after all, Nick," she said. "Mrs. Morison of the *Gazette* has given me a job."

"Mrs. Morison?" He looked at Steven, his thick brows raised inquiringly. "Your mother, right?"

"Yes," Steven said slowly, "but it's not what you think. Renée got this job on her own."

"I'm sure she did," Nick said coolly. "Well, I was coming in to say hello, but I'll see you later, Renée."

Before she could stop him, he went off down the street. His hands were stuffed in his pockets, and he held his head high.

For Renée the light, happy day had somehow turned cold and gloomy.

Steven glanced after Nick and turned back to her. "So that's Nick DiLeo," he said. "The fellow you once told me you were supposed to marry. Nick seems like a nice enough man, but I'm glad you're rid of him." Steven's burnished gold hair blew in the wind, and he laughingly pushed it back. "Now, maybe I'll have a chance."

She laughed, too. Steven had a way of restoring her good spirits. For a moment their eyes locked; then she abruptly swiveled around. "Good-night, Steven." She ran lightly up the steps.

"I'll see you at the *Gazette*," he called, but she was already closing the door.

In the next week she saw Steven twice, once to attend the theater to see the singer Lillian Russell, and the second time to go ice-skating. Megan joined them for skating, and although she was still wary of Renée, she asked a lot of questions and later invited her to lunch the following week.

Renée was elated. Now maybe she'd have a chance to become better acquainted with Steven's sister. So far, she'd never felt comfortable with Megan, but if they got to know one another, perhaps they'd become friends. And she did long for a girl-friend in whom she could confide.

The next morning, Saturday, as Renée shelled peas at the kitchen table with the sun streaming in, she thought of Steven. At times he could be serious, but at other times, teasing. Every time she was with him she liked him more. Was she falling in love? she wondered. No, she'd planned on a career, and not even love would stop her from attaining her goal. She was gaining good experience at the *Gazette*, despite the fact that Mr. Webb had assigned her to Miss Flora Blossom, the Food and Fashion editor. She'd asked Mr. Webb to place her with a roving reporter, and the memory of his derisive snort brought a flush to her cheeks. He'd said she'd be in the way with anyone except Miss Blossom. Obviously, the less he saw of her, the better he liked it. But she didn't let his dislike dampen her love for newspaper work. She kept her eyes and ears open, and each time she reported for work, she learned something new.

"I'm home," Olivia called, carrying two large loaves of Italian bread and a coffee cake. She stamped the snow off her boots and removed the scarf from her head. Placing the bakery goods on the table, she said, "Mr. DiLeo threw in a few molasses cookies, too."

"Aunt Olivia," Renée protested, setting the shelled peas in the sink, "you shouldn't spend your money on coffee cake."

"Nonsense," Olivia said. "It was fresh from the oven and I couldn't resist it. Besides, I love to buy for my family. Why should I hoard money? Now that I've put enough away for my funeral, I can spend a little."

"Aunt Olivia! Don't even think such a thing."

The older woman shrugged. "Life and death. Someday, death claims us all. It's natural." She sliced the bread for Tony's breakfast. "What do you plan to do on this fine Saturday, Renée?"

"Today I promised Tony I'd help him with his homework and tonight," she said casually, "I'm going out with Nick." She rinsed off the peas.

"Nick?" Olivia questioned. "Not Steven?"

"No-o-o," Renée said slowly. "Nick asked me a long time ago to attend a concert."

"I see," Olivia said, busying herself in setting the table.

"Hi," Tony said, rushing in and dropping in a chair. His small, bright face looked from one to the other. "I'm hungry," he said, hitching up a suspender.

"I've fixed oatmeal and toast for you," Renée said, setting a bowl before him.

She loved to watch Tony eat. He had lots of energy, and his thin, wiry body had shot up three inches in the past year.

"When do we start on my homework?" Tony asked between mouthfuls.

"When do you want to?" she countered.

"Soon as possible," he said, heaping jelly on his toast. "We're building a snow fort today. We challenged the kids on Seventy-third Street to a snowball fight."

"Just don't get hurt," Renée warned. "Mother has enough to do without worrying about you. Right now she's at Mrs. Poletti's. The poor woman's been sick and Mother took her a pot of minestrone soup."

"Last time those guys put stones in their snowballs and Dan got his face cut," Tony said, his thoughts still on the upcoming battle.

"Be careful," Renée warned.

"Aw, we gotta have some fun." His eyes twinkled, and he flashed a smile at Renée.

Renée reached over to tousle his already mussy hair, but he easily dodged away from her hand.

"Scoot," she ordered. "Comb your hair, wash your sticky fingers, and come back here with your books. We'll start on your reading assignment."

Renée cleared away the dishes and wiped the table clean. She wished she were going out with Steven tonight. She not only loved being with him, but it was fun to be picked up in a fancy carriage. Tonight she and Nick would take the horse-drawn streetcar. Since when, she thought, rubbing the tabletop harder, did taking the streetcar bother her? She glanced guiltily at Olivia, afraid her aunt could read her thoughts. But Olivia was peeling onions as she hummed to herself. Ah, Steven, Renée thought, he was not only rich, but supported her in her desire for a career. Nick no doubt sided with his father. But did he? She didn't know what he thought.

Filling the dishpan with sudsy water, she began to do the dishes. She tried to push thoughts of Steven and Nick out of her mind, but it didn't work.

In the soapsuds she saw first the image of Steven, then Nick. Why did life have to be so complicated? Well, she though grimly, scouring a frying pan, she had no room for romance at this time. No room at all.

Chapter Seven

AFTER the concert Renée and Nick stopped at a café for hot chocolate.

Nick, sitting across from her, said with a grin, "You're glowing, Renée." His even white teeth were in sharp contrast to his olive complexion. "Is it Steven Morison who's put the roses in your cheeks?"

She sipped her hot chocolate, studying Nick's face over the cup's rim. He was such a dear friend. And how good-looking he appeared in his striped suit. Did she dare confide in him?

"You can talk to me, Renée. You always have before," he urged. "Remember when we were little? We sat on the front stoop, talking for hours. You were seven and I was ten. I wanted to be a ship's captain, and you wanted to be a railroad engineer."

Her laughter tinkled like a wind chime. "We'd talk until dark. You told me I couldn't be a train engineer — that only men ran trains. So then I said I'd be a sea captain, like you, Nick, but you said I couldn't do that, either — that only men sailed ships. Finally, I asked you what was left for me to do."

"And I answered that you didn't have to *do* anything," Nick said, chuckling. "That I'd take care of you."

"I remember," she said softly.

"Nine years ago." Nick sighed, tugging at his collar. "You haven't changed much. You still want to go into a man's profession." He took her hand. "And I still feel the same way about you." He saw a shadow cross her face and held up his palms, hastening to reassure her. "I know you don't want anyone to take care of you, Renée. But," he said softly, "you can't stop me from loving you and wanting to marry you."

"A wedding would please our fathers, wouldn't it?" she asked teasingly, but with an undertone of bitterness.

"It *would* please our families," Nick admitted, his eyes a sober, dark hue, "but that has nothing to do with the way I feel about you. Someday I hope you'll love me as I love you. Until that someday," he said lightly, "I want you to work — and to be happy. I'd never stand in your way."

"Thanks, Nick," she said quietly. "Sometimes I feel like that same seven-year-old girl around you. No wonder I've always liked you and enjoyed being with you. I'm glad we can still talk."

"I want more than that." Nick's voice deepened. "I want your love. But," he added calmly, "I realize you need time." A mocking smile crossed his lips. "And Steven Morison has now entered the picture."

She nodded, yearning to reach out and touch his hand. Nick would always be special, yet she didn't want to offer false encouragement. Steven was very much in the picture. She and Nick had always been honest with one another and she couldn't promise him a love she didn't feel.

They walked home in a light falling snow, and she didn't mind when he held her hand.

And when they reached her home she didn't mind when he leaned down and kissed her cheek. "For old times' sake," he whispered.

Tears trembled on her lashes. "Good-night, Nick."

He gazed at her, then spun about. "Good-bye, Renée."

Transfixed, she watched him walk away. Was it good-bye? Good-bye to all their childish dreams? Good-bye to Nick? Sadly she went up the steps.

Frank was the only one still up when she came in.

"Hi," he said, taking off his policeman's helmet. "I just got in from my afternoon shift." He unbuttoned the long jacket of his blue uniform and went to the icebox. "How did you and Nick get along tonight?" he asked, glancing at her.

"Fine," she answered, not elaborating. She wondered if everyone in the family was waiting to see what she and Nick had decided.

Frank poured a tall glass of milk and sank down in a kitchen chair. "You haven't heard my news."

"What news?" she questioned.

"Rose and I have settled on our wedding date."

"That's wonderful," Renée said excitedly. "When is it?"

"June fifteenth. Rose wants you for a bridesmaid, but I'll let her fill you in on the details."

"I'm thrilled," she said, kissing the top of her brother's head. She liked Rose. Frank had been going with her for three years. "Father and Mother will be pleased."

"Rose and I will be moving into our own flat." He cocked his head, laughing. "They'll be glad to be rid of their twenty-year-old son."

"No, no," Renée protested. She added impishly, "With your wedding to plan, it will take their minds off me."

"I think Dad's right, you know," Frank said, finishing his milk. "You couldn't find a better man than Nick."

Not Frank, too, she thought glumly, but she added mildly, "I'm not ready for marriage yet, Frank." But silently she studied her brother. Of medium height, with a round face that was decorated with a brush mustache, long sideburns, and brown velvet eyes, he cut quite a dashing figure and could date anyone he wanted. Once he'd met Rose, however, he'd never gone with anyone else. Rose was a nice neighborhood girl whose parents owned the fruit market down the street. Their families got along well, and Frank was doing what was expected of him. Why did she have to be the contrary one?

Not wanting to pursue the discussion, she blew Frank a kiss. "I'm happy for you and Rose. I'll talk to Rose later about the wedding. Good-night, Frank."

On the following Saturday Renée met Megan at The Regal, a lovely café overlooking the park.

Megan, sitting at a window table, motioned to her.

Renée waved, hurrying forward. How lovely Megan looked, she thought. All sunshine yellow. Her dress and cape, in a marigold shade, was set off by a jaunty green velvet hat. Her blonde hair curled out from beneath the hat, which was tipped at a rakish angle.

"You look so pretty, Megan," Renée said with delight, slipping into the high-backed chair.

Megan smiled. "Thank you, Renée. So do you."

Renée laughed, feeling pretty and knowing that her jet-black hair contrasted sharply with Megan's. She enjoyed the heads that kept turning in their direction. "I've been shopping," Megan said, removing her elbow-length gloves. "There's so much to do before my wedding." She sighed, tilting her head for Renée's reaction.

"That's exciting," Renée said, thinking of Frank's June wedding. Was everyone in the world getting married except her?

"And I bought the most darling black lace peignoir set. . . ."

The waiter, a linen towel draped over one arm, appeared at their table.

"May I order for us?" Megan asked.

"Please." Renée was glad she didn't have to decipher the long menu.

As Megan quickly ordered, Renée was impressed with how easily she pronounced the French phrases.

After the waiter left, Renée inquired, "Who's the man you're going to marry, Megan?"

Megan smiled and closed her eyes. "His name's Charles Danziger the Third. He's a head taller than me; he has a mane of brown hair, a heavy beard, and hazel eyes." She paused as if visualizing her fiancé. "He's very self-possessed and has a reputation for being one of the most brilliant traders on Wall Street."

"Sounds wonderful. Where will you live?"

"Charles is building our new home directly opposite the Stewart mansion on Thirty-fourth Street and Fifth Avenue."

The waiter set an endive salad in front of them.

Renée nibbled on the pungent leaves and found that she liked them. "Is that the Stewart who owns the department store?"

"That's the one." Megan leaned forward. "I can't wait." And a radiant smile spread over her delicate features.

Renée smiled, too. Megan could be as cold and untouchable as a porcelain doll, but today she was warm and enchanting. Impulsively Renée asked, "Will you come to dinner at our house next Sunday?" She glanced around at the high ceiling, the tall windows and the potted plants. "It won't be quite as elegant as The Regal, however."

Megan's green eyes shone eagerly. "I'd love to. I've never been on Seventy-fourth Street."

Renée grinned. "It's not as bad as the Tenderloin district, if that's what you're thinking."

"I didn't mean . . ." Megan began, looking stricken.

Renée laughed. "I know you didn't."

"The food will be heavier than this," she said, picking at the few scallops on her silver-trimmed plate. "You'll meet my two brothers, Tony and Frank, my Aunt Olivia, and my parents. Oh, and Rose Rizzo, Frank's fiancée, will be there, too. She always comes on Sunday."

"It sounds like fun," Megan said, as if she were going on an adventure.

Renée picked up her crystal water glass and

hoped the dinner would be fun. She didn't exactly know what her family would think of Megan or how Megan would view her family. She only knew that she loved them, and if Megan found them too different and not to her taste, then that was her loss.

Chapter Eight

RENÉE helped Aunt Olivia and Mother prepare Sunday's dinner. She wanted everything to be perfect, and she polished the silver until it gleamed.

"Mother, I'll fold the napkins into a fan shape. That's the way they were fixed at The Regal."

"Go ahead," her mother said, giving her an exasperated look. "Just be certain you cut up all the vegetables for the chicken soup."

"But I need time to bathe and press my dress," Renée wailed. She knew Megan would be dressed in the latest fashion.

"Now, listen, young lady. You've been fussing over this dinner as if Queen Victoria were coming. Our Sunday dinners are always special and we're not changing things for your Fifth Avenue girl-friend."

Renée felt her cheeks redden. Did she sound like a snob? Why couldn't she just relax and treat this dinner as any other?

"Sorry, Mother," she murmured, not bothering to fold the napkins. Instead, she hurried to slice the vegetables. Megan would be here soon, and she'd just have to take the Conti family as they were.

When Megan arrived, everyone appraised her petite frame, from her red leather high-tops to her hat with its perky crimson feather. The family put on their best manners, and for a while the stilted atmosphere made Renée uncomfortable. Where was everyone's usual high spirits? Mrs. Conti, however, broke the spell. "John," she said dryly, "pull up a chair for our guest." She smiled at Megan. "May I offer you a glass of chianti?"

"Chianti?" questioned Megan, looking like a fashion model in her gray-plaid suit.

"It's mostly water with a splash of red wine," Aunt Olivia said with a chuckle.

"I'd love a glass."

As Mrs. Conti poured the wine, Megan admired Olivia's lace collar. "It's such fine work," she marveled.

"I tatted it," Olivia said simply, but her stern expression changed into a warm smile. She looked lovely, too, in the flickering gaslight, holding the ruby-colored wine.

John pulled forth his big chair for Megan, and Frank brought a footstool. Rose sat quietly on the sofa, but Tony, sitting cross-legged at Megan's feet, wasn't bashful. "Where do you live?" he asked, his black eyes studying her, "and where do you go to school?"

Megan laughed softly. "I live on Fifth Avenue, and I attend Miss Regina Loomis' School for Girls."

Soon Megan was answering other questions and was talking as if she were part of the family.

Renée was pleased that Megan didn't disappoint anyone after she'd described her in such glowing terms.

The meal was lively, with everyone talking and laughing at the same time. Renée was enjoying herself, too, especially when she heard Megan's laughter ripple across the table.

Mrs. Conti watched anxiously as Megan tasted her soup, and was delighted when she asked for seconds. She ate all her veal parmigiana, pasta, and custard pie. For such a petite girl she had a big appetite.

Megan was interested in everyone, questioning Frank about police work and Rose about their wedding. She tilted her head, her blonde curls in an upsweep with a few tendrils escaping onto her forehead, and said, "Mr. Conti, I'm delighted with my Safety bicycle, but I'm afraid I'll need a lesson or two."

"The Safety is the latest thing," Renée's father

said, beaming. "It was brought over from England a few months ago. The English have been riding it for two years."

"I've ridden it around our third-floor ballroom, but I'm so wobbly I've already fallen off twice." She giggled, holding a hand to her lips. "Renée, will you teach me?"

Renée nodded happily, pleased that Megan wanted her help. She was pleased, too, that everyone liked her. Even Aunt Olivia presented her with a lace collar, which Megan accepted with pleasure. She tied it over her blouse, and the stand-up collar set off her lovely features to perfection.

After she'd left, Mrs. Conti conceded that Megan was a lovely girl, and was glad Renée had her for a friend.

The next week at the *Gazette* Renée continued to learn from Miss Flora Blossom. She found out how to do a layout and how to cut and paste articles on social teas and weddings. By now she knew everyone in the newsroom and loved her job. However, she still stayed clear of Mr. Webb, who glowered at her every time she came near. She wondered why he was so antagonistic. Well, she thought, she had her own little niche in Miss Blossom's office and would do her work, and when she had time she'd visit with Louis Brown or James Tiller in the newsroom. These two reporters were always ready to share with her whatever they were doing.

One day Miss Blossom hurried into the office. "Renée," she said breathlessly, stabbing a hatpin into the hat that perched precariously on her brown braids, "I want you to finish the layout for the society page. I'm off to cover a wedding."

"Do you trust me to turn in the copy?" Renée asked, overjoyed, yet not quite believing her ears.

Miss Blossom's fingers fluttered lightly through a pile of papers on her desk. At last she pulled forth a list of names. "Don't worry, Renée, you'll do fine without me. So far you haven't made one mistake, and I depend on you." She buttoned her jacket, threw on her cape, pulled on her hat and said, "This Maller-Ferguson wedding is one of the biggest of the year." She paused, giving a gleeful chuckle. "Not as big, of course, as Grover Cleveland's wedding to Miss Folsom in June 1886."

"You went to the President's wedding?" Renée asked in awe.

"I was one of the lucky ones. There were only twenty-eight guests, but I was a friend of the bride's. Yes," she said cheerfully, "that was the highlight of my career. When forty-nine-year-old Grover married twenty-three-year-old Frances Folsom, it was the talk of the country. I took the train to Washington, D.C., and covered all the festivities."

"Were they married in the White House?"

"Oh, yes, in the Blue Room, to be precise. Frances was such a tall, willowy bride, and Grover was, well, he was a rather paunchy bridegroom. Frances didn't carry any flowers and the only jewelry she wore was a sapphire-and-diamond engagement ring. They're a good match," she hastened to add. "Frances is a wonderful hostess and a marvelous conversationalist. And they've already had a darling daughter. Oh, my," she said, looking at her pendant watch. "It's two o'clock. I must run. Mr. Webb wants the society page in by three. Can you manage that?"

"It's as good as done," Renée answered confidently. She'd observed Miss Blossom doing a mockup a hundred times.

After Flora Blossom bustled out, Renée rolled up her sleeves and set to work. Miss Blossom's desk was heaped high with notices of upcoming events and pictures, but it was amazing how Flora never had trouble finding anything. She'd pull out just the item she wanted from a sheaf of papers a foot high.

"Hello, Renée," Mr. Brown said, sticking his white head around the corner. "How ya doin'?"

"Fine," she answered with a smile, trying to clear the desk so that she could spread out the pictures.

"You're looking mighty pretty today."

"Why thank you, Mr. Brown. And what do you want to borrow today?" she asked, her smile broadening.

He chuckled. "Only the paste pot." He held up one hand with his fingers splayed. "Five minutes only!"

"Here," she said, handing him the white jar. "Are you working on a big story?"

"I'm doing an interview with J. P. Morgan in about two hours."

"The banker?" she asked incredulously.

"Banker, financier, and owner of railroads. He owns half the railroad mileage in the United States." Louis Brown lit his pipe, and for an instant the flame illumined his lined face.

"I've heard he's quite cantankerous." Renée gave him a mischieveous look. "But with your blarney, he'll give you all the information you need."

"I don't know," Mr. Brown said doubtfully. "J. P.'s curt and to the point. I'll have to pry details out of him." He laughed. "I met him once, and those piercing eyes of his and that enormous red, bulbous nose would frighten most people."

"But not you, right?"

"If a reporter's too scared, he won't get a good story."

"Or *she* won't get a good story," Renée said good-naturedly.

"I stand corrected." He gave a mock bow. "I'll bring this right back," he said, holding up the paste pot.

Renée commenced her work, arranging photos and the typed names beneath. The articles fit in nicely, and she only needed to add a few captions. It was almost three o'clock, and she wanted to be sure to meet Mr. Webb's deadline.

She had been so intense, she hadn't even heard Louis Brown bring back the paste pot, but she knew he had when she reached for it.

All at once the pot tipped over, the lid came off, and the paste oozed all over her fresh copy. "Oh, no," she groaned, dashing to find a rag to mop up the thick, white mess. Paste had dripped onto the pictures and several articles. In her haste to wipe up the paste, several pictures had fluttered to the floor.

Her heart was pounding as she picked up the sticky photos and placed them back in their slots. If she mixed up the wrong pictures with the wrong names, Miss Blossom would never forgive her.

"Where's the society page?" Mr. Webb shouted, striding into the office. "I need the — " Chomping on his cigar, he stopped in mid-sentence and removed the stogie. He stared at the paste seeping over the desk, too dumbfounded to speak.

"M-Mr. Webb," Renée stammered, her throat so dry she could barely get the words out. "I'll clean this up and the printer will be able to read the layout, I promise you."

"Who could read such muck!" He shook his head, his jowls shaking with anger. "I didn't want to hire you in the first place." He pointed his finger at the door and roared, "Get out! You're fired!"

Chapter Nine

STUNNED, Renée stood rooted to the spot, paste sticking to her hands and dripping onto her skirt.

"Didn't you hear me?" Mr. Webb thundered, his eyes blazing. "You're fired!" He thrust his bulldog face menacingly close to hers. "Out!"

"What is all this commotion?" Zena Morison asked as she stopped in the doorway and glanced quizzically from Mike Webb to Renée.

"Look at this mess," Mike Webb said, indicating the partially dried paste on the mock-up sheet.

Zena Morison came nearer and examined the page. "This can be salvaged. The printers have read worse than this."

"Renée Conti can't do one thing right!" he muttered, holding up the sticky page. "But, I agree," he said reluctantly. "It is readable." He stuck his head out the door and yelled, "Bill!"

A copyboy dashed in, and Mike handed him the sheet. "Get this up to the typesetters."

The boy gingerly took the paper and stared in bewilderment at the gooey clumps of paste.

"And step on it!" Mike growled.

"Yes, sir!" Bill answered, spinning about and rushing out.

"I promised Renée a three-month trial, Mike," Zena said mildly. "It was an honest mistake. Don't you think we could give her another chance?"

"All right," he grunted. "Two more months! Unless," he wagged a finger under Renée's nose, "she makes another mistake. Then it's out for good!"

"Fair enough, Mike," Zena agreed amiably. She tilted her head and glanced at Renée. "Is that all right with you, my dear?"

"Oh, yes, ma'am," she said. "And thank you, Mr. Webb. I'll be extra careful."

"You'd better be!" he grumbled, his eyebrows descending low over his still smoldering eyes. "Of all the stupid things!"

"I'm sorry," Renée repeated, throwing out her hands in a helpless gesture. "I don't know how it happened." But she did know. Louis Brown had returned the paste pot without firmly screwing on the lid. However, it was her fault, too, for not checking it. How could she blame Louis for her own carelessness?

Mike Webb frowned, saying between clenched teeth, "Just remember, young lady, you have only one more chance!"

"I won't forget," she said in a low, tight voice.

He glared at her for an instant, then jabbed his cigar in his mouth and strode away, muttering, "Dumb, dumb, dumb."

Zena looked at Renée reproachfully. "I don't like to undermine Mr. Webb's authority, but in this instance I think I was justified." She gave her a quick smile. "Don't make another mistake, Renée, because next time I won't interfere. Is that clear?"

"I understand," Renée answered meekly. "And I'll try not to make any more blunders."

"Good," Zena said briskly. "Clean up the spilled paste and go on home for the day."

"Yes, Mrs. Morison," she said gratefully. When she was alone, she took a shaky breath. Tears sprang to her eyes as she began to scrub the desktop. One more mistake! Would she be able to last for two months, she wondered grimly. She rather doubted it, with Mr. Webb scrutinizing her every move!

For the next few weeks Renée was extra careful not to make an error, and fortunately her life did settle into a normal routine. She saw Steven every Saturday night and on Valentine's night, there was a special treat. He was taking her to Buffalo Bill's Wild West Show. She was eager to see the performance that had been such a smash hit in London, impressing Queen Victoria, herself!

That night Steven picked her up in his carriage, and when they entered Madison Square Garden, she wasn't surprised that he had reserved front row center seats.

Renée clapped her hands to see stagecoaches being held up and mock Indian attacks repulsed with roaring gunfire. Annie Oakley, a star of the show, fired a rifle at dimes tossed in the air, hitting them with stunning accuracy. Renée had never seen such a superb markswoman, but it was little wonder, she thought, for Annie had been trained to shoot since childhood. After "Little Sure Shot's" target exhibition, William F. Cody, former pony express rider and buffalo hunter, introduced Chief Sitting Bull, the Indian chief who led the attack on General Custer's troops at Little Bighorn. For the exciting finale all the stars rode out, taking a final bow.

Nothing, however, was as exciting as the valentine Steven presented to her on the way home.

"Here is your valentine," he said. Then he drew out from beneath the seat a lacy box adorned with two turtledoves and papier-mâché roses. With a flourish, he handed her the heart-shaped box saying, "This is for you, Renée."

She sucked in her breath as she opened the beautiful box, trailing with pink ribbons. Assorted chocolates filled the box.

"So you'll never forget me," he said.

She glanced at him, a teasing smile on her lips. "Every time I eat a chocolate I'll think of you."

"Take that big chocolate in the corner," he urged.

She laughed. "I couldn't possibly eat all of this." But when she picked it up, she discovered the chocolate was really a small brown velvet box. Gently she opened the lid and inside, on a bed of white satin, was a tiny gold heart. "Steven," she said softly, as she held up the lovely pendant. It shimmered in the moonlight as it swung to and fro on its delicate golden chain.

"Like it?" he said hopefully.

"I love it," she whispered.

"Let me fasten the clasp for you," he offered, taking the fine chain and leaning close.

The necklace gleamed against her dark dress. "Thank you," she murmured.

Steven pressed her to him and gently kissed her. "Happy Valentine's Day, Renée," he said softly.

"Oh, Steven," she said, "you're so sweet."

"I'll always be sweet to you, sweetheart." His green eyes sparkled like emeralds in the cold silver light.

Then Steven rested his face against her hair and said in a low voice, "I love you, Renée."

"Dear Steven," she said, not knowing what to reply. At this moment she felt affection for him but was reluctant to express her feelings. "I don't know what to say. . . ."

"Don't say anything. I want lots of time to prove my love to you. I want to show you a side of New York you've never seen. We'll eat caviar, go for hansom rides around Central Park, dance at the Barkley and . . ."

She laughed softly. "Stop, stop, Steven, you're filling my head with all kinds of wonderful images. I feel like I'm in a dream, and tomorrow I'll wake up."

But in the morning she knew it wasn't a dream when she looked in the mirror and touched the golden heart at her throat. Her eyes were luminous and her skin smooth and rosy. She was so happy she almost floated into breakfast. Was this what being in love felt like?

"You got in late last night and didn't have time to see the mail," Tony teased with a sassy smile on his face. "You've got a valentine!"

"A valentine?" Renée asked, bewildered.

"Yes," Mrs. Conti said. "Why do you look so puzzled? Have you forgotten Nick already?"

Renée blushed. Of course. Nick. Embarrassed, she looked at the huge envelope that Tony had propped up against her glass.

"Open it. I want to see what he sent you." He grinned. "I'll bet it's got cupids and ribbons and flowers and a lovey-dovey verse."

"You'll be late for school," Renée warned.

"I want to see your valentine!"

"If you scat," she said, "I'll give you two chocolates when you get home this afternoon."

"Oh, all right!" Tony said, wrinkling up his nose. "I didn't want to see your gooey valentine, anyway." Suddenly his puckish face was sunny again. "Don't forget the chocolates!" And with a gleeful shout he picked up his book bag and ran out the door.

Renée stared at the envelope and glanced at her mother, then back at Nick's valentine. Unfolding the flap, she pulled out a beautiful fan with pictures of young girls framed in hearts. The flower-trimmed fan had the simple words: "To my sweetheart. Please take my heart. Nick."

Hastily she folded up the gilt-ribbed fan and tucked it into her pocket.

Her mother, setting down a plate of hot blueberry muffins, frowned at Renée. "You mustn't lead Nick on, Renée. I think Steven is getting serious, and Nick is, too. You should make up your mind."

"Mother," she protested. "I'm only sixteen." But the memory of being with Steven the night before sent a warm feeling through her.

"You should tell Nick to see other girls," Mrs. Conti said matter-of-factly. "I can see that Steven has a special place in your heart."

"I will," Renée promised. But the image of Nick with another girl caused her stomach to knot.

"I-I'm not hungry," she said quickly, rising and kissing her mother's cheek. "I've got to get to school early," she lied.

After school Renée went directly to the *Gazette*, where she began proofreading galleys. How lucky she was, she thought, that Flora Blossom still trusted her after the paste fiasco.

"Hello, dear," Flora said, walking in. "I've just received the recipes from the Staten Island Women's Club. We're going to have a whole section in Monday's paper on German cooking." She riffled through several recipes, talking to herself. "Marinated beef, Thuringers, Wiener schnitzel, apple strudel . . ."

"Stop!" Renée said with a laugh. "You're making me hungry!"

Flora glanced up. "Sorry." Suddenly she placed her hand against her cheek. "Oh, dear, I forgot. Mrs. Morison wanted to see the copy on the Beninger reception. Take these in to her, will you, Renée?"

"Of course," she said, gathering up the long sheets and hurrying to Zena Morison's office.

Pausing, she straightened the sheets before she went in. All at once she heard Megan's voice and was going to step in and greet her when she heard her name spoken.

"Renée is a nice girl, Mother," Megan said, "and I *do* like her, but what about poor Alicia? Steven has taken her out for the past year and now Renée steps in and Alicia's no longer around."

"Steven hasn't seen Alicia Totten recently, has

he?" Zena Morison said thoughtfully. "But I can see why Steven likes Renée. She's not only beautiful and sparkling but she has a good head on her shoulders as well."

"I know," Megan replied, "but don't you think Steven should stick to girls in his own social class? After all, he'll be a Harvard graduate and own a newspaper. Besides, Alicia's beautiful, too. And her father owns a steamship company."

Zena sighed audibly. "Sometimes you can be quite a snob, Megan, but I know you want only what's best for your brother. . . . Maybe you're right, I don't know."

"Steven rushes into things," Megan said, "and I think . . ."

But Renée didn't wait to hear what Megan thought. She turned away, her eyes moist and her knees trembling. Whatever made her think she was right for Steven? When the copyboy went by, she called, "Bill," her voice almost a croak. "Bill," she repeated, steadying herself, "would you give this copy to Mrs. Morison?"

"Sure thing," Bill replied and peered at her anxiously. "Are you all right, Miss Conti?"

"I'll be fine," she said shakily. Her stomach churned as she stumbled toward Miss Blossom's office. What a fool she'd been, she thought. Choking back bitter tears, she realized she'd never be accepted by the Morisons.

Chapter Ten

FOR the next two weeks Renée always had an excuse when Steven asked her out. At first he'd been puzzled and tried to coax her to see him, but she had remained firm. Megan's words still rang in her head. "Steven should stick to girls in his own social class." Perhaps her father was right after all, Renée thought, and she should marry Nick, a boy of her own background.

But she didn't see much of Nick, either. Instead, she studied her English and history, analyzed newspaper articles, and read William Dean Howells, Mark Twain, and Henry James. Some nights she couldn't sleep. It made her sad to have to give up Steven. And poor Steven didn't know why she no longer wanted to see him. Did he believe she'd lost interest? She should be honest and tell him her feelings. But how could she? She didn't believe what Megan had said. She was every bit as good as Megan and this Alicia she'd mentioned.

But she was lonely without Steven and did everything she could to forget him.

One night when she and her father were drawing up an order for bicycle parts, Nick came by.

"Hello, everyone," he said, going over to Tony, who sat at the other end of the table doing homework, and playfully thumped his arm.

"Hi, Nick," Aunt Olivia said, seated by the gas lamp with Blackie in her lap. She didn't drop a stitch from the afghan she was knitting. "Nice to see you."

Nick looked at Renée. "Home on a Saturday night?" he asked quizzically, his thick black brows arching.

"I'm home," she said, "but keeping busy." She kept her pencil poised over the long list. She didn't want him to think she didn't have anything to do.

"Come in, Nick. Come in and sit down, my boy," John Conti said jovially. "You've been a stranger lately."

"I've been busy, too," he said lightly, his dark eyes fastened on Renée.

"Nick, will you help me with my arithmetic?" Tony said, tapping his pencil on the table.

John Conti laughed. "I don't think Nick came over to see you, Tony." He winked at Renée.

Flustered, she said, "Would you like a cup of coffee, Nick?"

"I thought perhaps we could go for a walk instead," he answered, a boyish smile softening his lips. "We can stop in at Vecchio's Pharmacy for a soda."

She hestitated. "I'd better not. I'm helping Father go over an order."

"Go on, go on," urged John Conti. "I'll finish this."

"You're sure?" Nick asked.

John chuckled. "You two go out and have a good time."

"But Father, we're almost finished," Renée protested.

"Nonsense," he said, shaking his head. "Don't you think I can put together an order? What do you think I've been doing while you've been working at the *Gazette*?"

"All right," she answered doubtfully. She glanced at Nick, and when he flashed his irresistible grin at her, she gave him a warm smile in return. "I'll get my coat, Nick." It was almost March, with winter almost over, and she'd barely seen him. She'd enjoy having a talk.

Once outside, their boots squeaked on packed-down snow, while the night air, brisk and windy, made her shiver. "I-I'm cold," she said between chattering teeth.

Nick grabbed her hand. "Let's run," he said, pulling her along.

They arrived at Vecchio's, laughing and out of breath. A chocolate soda would taste good.

Nick ordered for them, and when the waiter brought the sodas, they didn't talk for a while. It was a comfortable silence.

Renée swirled the straw around in the last of her chocolate soda.

Nick leaned back, gazing at her. "Papa is opening another bakery on Second Avenue, a big, expensive one, and I'm to be the manager."

"You are?" she said, her eyes widening.

He laughed. "I love to see those eyes of yours get bigger and bluer. Yes," he went on. "I'll have the responsibility for the carriage trade. It will mean longer hours and baking more tortes and petit fours. Fancy pastries at fancy prices. And if I don't succeed, I'll be right back on Seventy-fourth Street."

"Nick, you'll make it. I know you will."

"You always have believed in me, Renée," he said quietly, his eyes warm. "And you?" he asked. "Do you intend to keep working at the *Gazette*?"

"Y-yes, I do," she said hesitantly. "As long as I can stay, with Mr. Webb breathing down my neck." She told him about the spilled paste and Mrs. Morison's intervention. "So, you see, Nick, Mr. Webb wants to fire me, and he's just waiting for an excuse."

"You'll prove how indispensable you are," he said reassuringly. "You'll be fine."

"You always did believe in me," she teased, echoing his words.

"Have since I was nine years old," he said, chuckling. His expression grew solemn. "And Steven Morison?" he questioned.

She yearned to tell Nick about Megan's remark, yet something held her back. Was she too ashamed to admit what Megan had said of her?

"Are you still seeing Steven?" Nick persisted gently.

"Not as frequently," she hedged. "My schoolwork and job have been keeping me busy."

He gave her a quizzical look but didn't pursue the topic.

"When does the new bakery open?" she asked, changing the subject.

"The end of March. The ovens and counters are going in next week."

Her mother's words echoed in her ears: "You should tell Nick to see other girls." She studied her empty soda glass, then gazed up at Nick's handsome face. Determinedly, she plunged forward. "Nick, I think you should take out someone else. Don't wait for me." Her words were forced and choked, barely audible. "It's not fair to — "

He grabbed her hand, almost fiercely. "Quiet," he said. "If I want to see another girl I will, but right now I'm as busy as you are. Besides, going out with someone else doesn't appeal to me. Maybe one day, but not now. . . ."

She breathed a sigh of relief. She didn't want him to see anyone else. He still loved her! For some reason that made her heart skip. Then she thought of Steven and guiltily jumped to her feet. "It's late," she said. "I have to get home."

Again he shot her a puzzled look but said nothing. Wordlessly, he wrapped her coat around her and rested his hands lightly on her shoulders.

With trembling fingers she fastened the buttons while Nick tied his muffler around his throat. As they walked home, her conflicting emotions collided with one another. The evening had been special. She hadn't realized how much she'd missed Nick's friendly face and reassuring words. Yet at times that night, even when she was talking to Nick, Steven's image hovered before her eyes.

After she'd said good-night, she stepped inside the quiet house. While she turned down the gas jets, two words echoed repeatedly in her mind — Steven-Nick-Nick-Steven.

After school the next day Renée prepared a layout on new spring suits.

"Renée, how are you?" Megan asked, poking her head in. She wore a sweet smile and for a moment Renée almost forgot the bitter words she'd overheard. How could Megan look all golden and lovely and speak to her in such a friendly way, after what she'd said about her?

"I'm fine," Renée answered coolly.

"Oh," Megan said, spying the fashion page.

"Aren't those suits scrumptious?" She came around the desk to have a closer look. "I like that one, don't you?" she asked, pointing to a black gabardine with a huge white collar and high white cuffs. "Which one do you like, Renée?"

But Renée busied herself with placing captions beneath the pictures and readying the display for Miss Blossom's finishing touch.

"I see you're busy, Renée," Megan said with a bright smile, "so I won't bother you, but let's get together soon."

Renée stared up at her, unable to utter a word. Oh, the falseness behind those clear green eyes!

With a cheerful wave Megan left. Her outward show of genuine friendship amazed Renée. Well, she remembered Megan telling her mother that she liked Renée, but that she just didn't belong to the right social class. Renée guessed you could "like" someone as long as you didn't have to associate with them too closely.

Megan had no sooner left than Steven stopped by. Renée's eyes froze on his long, slender form as he leaned casually against the doorjamb. He folded his arms and studied her. Flustered, she lowered her eyes and continued to rearrange the display.

Finally he said teasingly, "That's what I like to see. The help diligently working for the newspaper."

"Yes, I guess I am the 'help.' " She tossed back her head in a gesture of defiance. "And," she said lightly, "employers shouldn't mingle with employees."

Steven straightened up and his expression grew serious. "Is that why you haven't been seeing me lately?"

"I've been busy," she fibbed. "Between school and work I don't have much time left."

"I stopped by to give you this." He handed her an embossed envelope.

Opening the flap, she glanced up at him, wondering what it was.

Scanning the words, she was astonished to read:

Mr. Steven Morison
respectfully requests the company of
Miss Renée Conti
at the Cotillion Ball
on March 3rd, 1888.
Place: Edgewood Country Club.
Time: Nine o'clock.

Renée held the invitation with trembling hands. If only he knew how she'd love to go. But it wouldn't be right. Not when she knew how Megan and maybe even Mrs. Morison, felt about her. With a tremulous smile she thrust out the invitation to give it back to him and shook her head.

Chapter Eleven

"**Y**OU don't want to go to the Cotillion?" Steven stared, complete surprise on his face. "It's the fanciest ball of the season," he said, ignoring the invitation she held out to him. "I want you to go with me," he said softly, touching her wrist.

And what about Alicia Totten? she thought gloomily. But, recalling a conversation with him sometime before, she knew he hadn't hidden anything from her. There had been a girl, he confided, but nothing serious. So even if Megan considered Alicia Totten to be a serious girlfriend, Steven did not. Suddenly she straightened her shoulders and smiled at him. She wanted to attend the dance and she didn't care about Megan or Alicia. She only knew that she could hold her own with any of the finishing school girls.

"I'd love to go, Steven," she said with a smile, as she drew her hand back and tucked the invitation into her pocket. So, she thought, I'm actually going to a grand ball with Steven. She lifted her chin defiantly and wondered what Megan would say to that! Renée would love to see her face when Steven told her.

"Wonderful!" Steven said, gazing down at her. His green eyes were warm and inviting. "I'll pick you up at eight o'clock on Saturday. Wear the necklace I gave you, will you?"

"Yes, yes, I will," she responded happily.

"People will wonder who that gorgeous brunette is whom Steven Morison has on his arm," Steven said, a smile beneath his words. He blew her a kiss with the departing words, "And wear your prettiest gown."

She froze, staring at the empty doorway. A dress! She didn't have a dress to wear! What was she going to do? She dropped into her chair, pulled out the invitation, and reread it. The fanciest ball of the season, and the only good clothes she owned were a suit and a new bicycle dress. Slowly she crumpled up the invitation and threw it on the desk. Perhaps, she thought, tears stinging her eyes, she couldn't go after all.

On her way out Megan stopped in again. When she saw the wrinkled invitation and Renée's stricken face, she rushed to her side. "What's wrong, Renée?"

Renée hastily brushed aside her tears and turned her face away. "Nothing," she said as casually as possible. "Nothing at all." Oh, why didn't Megan leave her alone and go away!

Megan picked up the crumpled invitation and stared at Renée. "I just saw Steven," she said wonderingly. "He's so glad you agreed to go to the ball with him. Don't you want to go?" she asked, a bewildered expression on her face. "You'll love the affair. We do all the latest dances — the cakewalk, the cotillion — " She giggled. " 'Cotillon' is the French word for 'petticoat.' Maybe they call it that because petticoats fly when you step to the lively music." She peeked at Renée's face, hoping to coax a smile.

Renée said nothing, looking at Megan with round eyes. A new horror had unfolded. She not only didn't have anything to wear, but she didn't know any of the dances! "I'm not going," she said flatly.

"Why ever not? You'll be so beautiful." Megan smiled. "You and Steven will be the most handsome couple there!"

Renée shot her a bitter look. It must be nice to be rich and not have to worry about clothes or how to act or how to dance.

Megan tilted her head. "You'll be lovely in a pale yellow or beige gown." She caught her breath as a look of understanding swept over her face. Then she rushed on quickly. "I have just the dress for you. It's ivory satin, with the new mutton sleeve and green bows down the front."

Renée stared at her, unable to speak. At last she said coolly, "I shouldn't have accepted. I'll be out of place." She wanted to add, "And not only that. I'm not of Steven's social class, either." But she wouldn't fling Megan's words back in her face. Instead, she went on, "I don't know the cakewalk or the cotillion or whatever else they dance."

"I'll teach you," Megan said eagerly. "Why don't you come over after work, pick up the dress, and have your first dance lesson?"

Renée's brain was in a whirl. Was Megan doing this to transform Renée Conti, poor Cinderella, into a princess? Was this only sport for her? Or was she doing it because she really liked her? She wanted to believe it was because Megan was her friend. Yet doubts plagued her. Maybe Megan was helping her for her brother's sake. This way, Steven wouldn't be embarrassed. She did want to attend the Cotillion, however, and Megan had offered to help. She would accept graciously and not worry about Megan's motives. A sudden smile lit her face. "I'll be over at six, and," she added, "thanks."

Megan laughed. "It will be fun. See you later." With a flounce of her skirts she was gone.

Renée sank back in her chair, trying to fathom what had just taken place. Megan had once said those awful words, comparing her to Alicia. Yet were they so awful? If Alicia was a friend of Megan's, then you couldn't blame her for wanting Steven to continue seeing her. And just because Megan was helping her with the dance, didn't mean for one minute that Megan had changed her mind about her. Megan would never consider her as a serious rival for her brother's affection.

The week went fast. Aunt Olivia fitted the dress Megan had loaned her, and Renée practiced the dance steps Megan had taught her.

When Steven came to pick her up, she felt lovely, knowing that the ivory gown brought out the sapphire-blue of her eyes and gave her peach-tinted complexion a glow.

Steven, as usual, talked to everyone, asking Mr. Conti about the bicycle business; telling Mrs. Conti she looked pretty; checking on Olivia's handiwork; joking with Frank; and teasing Tony.

Once in the carriage, Steven leaned over, took her gloved hand, and said, "You look like a princess."

"And you, Steven," she said with a smile, her eyes twinkling, "look like a prince."

He threw back his head and laughed. "We're royalty going to a ball."

She laughed, too. But Steven really did look like an aristocrat in his dark tails, starched high collar, and black cravat. He wore white gloves, and his blond hair gleamed like spun gold in the shaft of moonlight that filtered in through the carriage window.

Entering the ballroom, which was glittering with chandeliers containing hundreds of Edison's new electric lights, Renée was filled with excitement. The sweet music, handsome couples, beribboned ceiling, sparkling punch glasses, and polished dance floor all added to her enchantment.

Steven seemed to know everyone, as he stopped to introduce her to this person and that couple.

When the orchestra's violins tuned up, Renée knew the dance was about to begin. Nervously she closed her fingers around the necklace Steven had given her and wondered if she'd know what to do after only three dance lessons.

But after Steven took her in his arms and swept her onto the floor, she followed his strong lead with easy grace. She loved the Boston, a slow, gliding dance patterned after the waltz, and she felt as if she were floating.

Next came a lively polka, and Renée's feet moved in fast steps as Steven twirled her around. She loved dancing. When the cotillion began, she rested her hands lightly on Steven's shoulders. She felt confident, having studied the directions in *Godey's Lady Book*, and self-assuredly faced Steven, who was opposite her in the men's line.

At the end of the music, the orchestra leader suddenly announced, "The cakewalk."

Renée removed a lacy white handkerchief from

her sleeve. Embroidered in the corner was a large butterfly with the initial "R" between its wings. Daintily, she touched the linen square to her forehead.

"Not the cakewalk," Steven groaned. "How about a glass of punch?"

She laughed. "You read my mind. I'm ready for a rest." But all at once the beat of the drum halted her. She paused, her hand on Steven's arm. The dancers moved onto the floor doing a high step. One couple came gliding onto the floor, followed by Megan and her partner.

"Steven," she exclaimed. "Look at your sister!"

"Yes, she and Charles are excellent dancers."

Megan lifted her skirts, and between the lines of hand-clapping onlookers, she and Charles high-stepped to the music. They did a fast slide and a few breathtaking leaps, followed by another couple who did even more intricate turns. Yet, another couple tried to outdo the first two.

Astonished, Renée watched Megan. She had no idea the demure blonde girl could be so lively and step so high.

"I'd love to learn that dance," Renée said.

"I'll teach you," Steven offered, "right after I bring you some refreshments. Stay here; I'll be right back."

While waiting, Renée tapped her toe to the music's beat, but a touch on her shoulder stopped her. Megan, a smile on her face and several curls tumbling free on her forehead, said breathlessly, "Renée, here's someone I want you to meet. This is Charles Danziger, my fiancé. Charles, meet Renée Conti."

Charles leaned down and kissed her hand. "My pleasure," he said. "I've heard a lot about you, Miss Conti." His hazel eyes shone with amusement in a lean face with a thick, full beard.

Another couple came off the floor, and Megan grabbed the girl's arm. "Renée, here's a friend of mine I want you to met. Alicia Totten, meet Renée Conti."

Renée stood very still, observing a tall, thin girl who now came forward and held out a gloved hand. Her head, atop a long slender neck, was small with a pile of curls on the top. She wore a yellow silk gown, decorated with jet-black beaded flowers, and she had a plume in her rich brown hair.

She arched her brows, smiled briefly, and coolly shook Renée's hand. "How nice to meet you, Renée."

Her blue eyes, a pale imitation of Renée's deep sapphire ones, were appraising. All of a sudden Renée no longer felt like a beautiful princess. She felt shy and awkward beside this regal beauty.

When Steven brought a cup of punch, Renée took it but didn't drink.

Alicia looped her arm through Steven's and said with a pretty pout, "I haven't danced with you all evening."

"May I?" Steven said, taking Alicia's hand. "Excuse me," he said to Renée and led Alicia onto the floor.

Renée sat the cup down. So this was her competition. Alicia was polished and sure of herself, obviously born to high society.

But Renée didn't ponder Alicia's background or her relationship to Steven for very long, because a young man asked her to dance.

When she glided to the lilting strains of a Strauss waltz, she forgot all about Alicia. She could become accustomed to this kind of life. The glitter and gaiety drew her like a magnet.

Chapter
Twelve

As Renée and Steven were getting ready to leave the ball, Steven's mother hurried over.

"Sorry I didn't get a chance to talk to you," Mrs. Morison said, "but the ballroom is so large and crowded that I only caught a glimpse of you during the evening." She adjusted the pink feather boa she wore around the neck of her crimson gown.

"It's so nice to see you, Mrs. Morison," Renée said, genuinely pleased she had come over.

"Come here, my dear," Zena said, drawing Renée over by a potted palm. She opened her fan and, holding it to her face, said in a low voice, "How would you like to write up tonight's ball?"

Renée almost shouted aloud. "I'd love to," she

said, too taken aback to say anything else. It would be her first article for the *Gazette*.

"Then it's settled," Zena Morison said, snapping shut her fan. "When you bring in your article on Monday, I'll help you with the names of a few illustrious guests. Robert Todd Lincoln and his wife, for example, were here, and so was Roscoe Conkling, the former senator from New York. Your article will be a short one for the society page." She tapped Renée's wrist with her fan. "Do a good job, Renée, and there might be other assignments." With these words she lifted her feather-trimmed skirt and moved briskly toward a bewhiskered gentleman.

"Mother really lets people know that the one year's mourning period for Father is over," Steven said. "A red dress!" he said with a smile and shake of his head.

On the way home, Renée told Steven about her assignment and then sank back against the horsehair seat, reveling in her good fortune. Already she planned what to write about. As soon as she got home, she'd jot down all her impressions so she wouldn't forget a thing.

Steven snapped his fingers before her eyes. "Remember me?" he said with a low chuckle. "I wish you were as dreamy-eyed over me as you are about writing an article."

"Sorry, Steven," Renée said, giving him an apologetic smile. "I guess I was thinking too much about my first byline."

"It's all right, Renée. I know you're excited." Casually he put his arm around her, and she leaned back contentedly.

"Oh, Steven, you've given me such a wonderful evening. I had such a good time."

"And everyone kept asking about you, Renée. They wanted to know all about the stunning girl I was escorting."

"And you told them I was a little girl from East Seventy-fourth Street," she said mischievously.

He laughed. "Oh, Renée, we're going to have such marvelous times together." His tone became serious. "Mother is managing the paper just fine, so I'll be able to return to Harvard soon. But I'll be back between terms, and when I do, I'd like to think you'll be waiting — that you'll be my girl. Will you do that?"

She hesitated, not wanting to commit herself. "I'll be here," she said thoughtfully, "and I'd love to go out with you, Steven."

"But will you be my girl?" he persisted.

"My newspaper work comes first. I can't think about a steady beau just yet," she answered softly. "Try to understand, Steven."

"You'll have a job at the *Gazette* for as long as you want, but once we're engaged," he cautioned, "you won't have much time. Oh, you can help Miss

Blossom when she needs you, but I'll be your first responsibility."

"Engaged?" Renée said, her heart leaping. To be engaged to Steven Morison! But the memory of his next words made her uncomfortable. "What do you mean when you say that my first responsibility is you?"

He grinned, and his teeth shone white in the coach's dark interior. "Just that. I don't want you to work full-time." His eyes sparkled as he kissed her fingertips. "I want you with me. Would that be such a terrible fate?" he teased.

"It would be a lovely fate," she bantered. "But let's enjoy each other. After you graduate we'll have time to talk about an engagement." She laughed. "Besides, what would your mother and Megan say?"

"What do you mean?" Steven said, puzzled. "They'd be thrilled, of course."

Renée smiled. Steven was so much in love he didn't realize Megan's concerns. But now wasn't the time to discuss them. She had an article to write, and when the carriage stopped, she didn't ask Steven to come in. She was too eager to start on her assignment, even if it was one o'clock in the morning.

On Sunday the whole family went to visit the Pelottis, except for Aunt Olivia and Renée. She had rewritten the Cotillion article four times.

"Aunt Olivia," she asked, putting a comma in a sentence. "What do you think of this?"

Aunt Olivia, sitting in the rocking chair, cocked her head as she listened to Renée's words. When Renée finished reading, Olivia said, "That sounds fine. I'm sure Mrs. Morison will accept it."

The quiet afternoon and the comfort of sitting with her aunt created a perfect time to talk, Renée thought. On an impulse she confided to Olivia about Steven's plans for the future.

Aunt Olivia stopped rocking and leveled her gaze on Renée. "Do you love Steven?" she questioned softly.

"I-I don't know," Renée answered truthfully. "I think so."

"You must be certain. You've already given up Nick. Why are you so quick to leap into an engagement with Steven?"

"But I wouldn't be rushed. Steven has to finish school. It's not the same as marrying Nick in one year, like Father wanted."

"And will Steven understand when you want to work on his newspaper? And will you be comfortable working for your fiancé?"

"I'd get another job," Renée countered. "One with the *Herald* or the *Times*." But it wasn't just the potential conflict of husband and wife working at the same place that bothered her. It was Steven's words that haunted her. "I'll be your first responsibility, Renée," he had said. Hopelessly, she threw her article on the table. "I don't know what to do."

"Do just what you're doing now," Aunt Olivia retorted. "You love your work, and you don't have to make any promises. Right now Steven has shown you a side of life that's rich and exciting, but you've worked too hard convincing your father to give you this chance. Don't throw it away."

Renée rose and kissed her Aunt Olivia's hollow cheek. "And you worked to give me this chance, too. Thanks for listening. I'll work this out. As long as I can talk to someone, it helps."

The next day Renée placed her article on Mrs. Morison's desk and was pleased she liked it. Except for inserting several prominent names, Mrs. Morison left the copy as it was.

Renée was so proud to see her name beneath an article.

As she went by Mr. Webb's office, she half expected him to compliment her on her first byline, but she should have known better. When he glanced her way, he then abruptly turned his head. He didn't bother to say hello or nod, she thought sourly. Well, she couldn't worry about him every minute. At least Miss Blossom was pleasant and gave her lots of encouragement.

For the next few days she thought of Steven's proposal. The future with Steven would be an exciting one, but nothing could be more exciting than newspaper work. And if he didn't want her to work full-time, her dream would come to an end. Soon he'd be going back to college and things would change. Maybe he'd even *want* her to become a journalist. Oh, to have Steven and be a newspaper reporter at the same time would be wonderful!

"Stop daydreaming," growled Mr. Webb, who stuck his head in the door. "There's no time for lollygagging around her."

She hurriedly grabbed a pencil and pad. "Sorry," she mumbled.

"Sorry," he mimicked. "That's not good enough, little lady. Just remember — one more mistake, and you're out of here!"

"Yes, sir," she replied, keeping her eyes cast down until he'd left.

For the rest of the week she worked diligently, hoping to impress Mr. Webb, but nothing she did brought one favorable remark.

She was happy to see Saturday, a sunny March 10th, arrive. Renée hummed as she put on her bicycle dress. Steven was coming at two o'clock, and she didn't want to be late. As she adjusted her striped yellow-and-red stockings, she heard Nick at the door. Usually she ran out to greet him, but today she sank into a chair before her heavy oak dresser. Rigidly she sat and combed her long hair, afraid Nick might ask her to go out for a soda again. With a pang she remembered the good time they'd recently had together and she didn't want to resurrect their warm relationship. It was easier not to face him. "Tell Renée I dropped by to see her," Nick said, his voice husky. There was a pause. "Here's something for you, Mrs. Conti. Cinnamon rolls fresh from the oven. Hope you like them."

Renée had the sneaking suspicion the rolls were for her.

"Thank you, Nick, you're a dear boy," Mrs. Conti answered lightly as if she, too, realized the small gift was for her daughter. "Come in and sit down."

"Sorry," Nick said, "but we're working today on our new Second Avenue bakery. The grand opening is April third."

Renée heard him clear his throat. "Tell Renée I dropped by." The door closed and he was gone.

Renée looked in the mirror, hating the image of the selfish girl staring back at her. Why hadn't she spoken to Nick? She had no reason not to, except that seeing him would have made her uncomfortable.

She pulled on her elbow-length kid gloves and determinedly dismissed all thoughts of Nick DiLeo. Coming out into the parlor, she felt wonderful in her bicycle dress with the matching knee bloomers, like a daffodil, all pert and yellow. The day was warm and balmy, with temperatures in the fifties, and Steven was riding over on his two-seater bicycle. They planned to bike to Central Park and then have dinner.

Steven was on time, looking dapper in his knickerbocker suit.

When they arrived at the park, an organ-grinder was standing on the corner. He played a silver-and-ivory barrel organ, and broke into an Italian love song while his monkey held out a tin cup. Steven cheerfully tossed a dime in it as they went by.

They biked past Central Park's zoo into a wooded area where a bicycle cop burst out of the brush, zooming after them. When he caught up, he warned them not to exceed the speed limit because he'd already given a couple of "scorchers" a ticket. They promised to slow down and went on past a stand of maple trees. Soon small buds would be on the branches, and Renée gloried in how green the grass would become. Spring would renew the park, and Renée tingled with joy. What a pleasure to be biking once again, and it was a double pleasure to be with Steven.

After an hour in the park, they headed down Fifth Avenue, pedaling past the Metropolitan Museum of Art, magnificent turreted mansions, St. Patrick's Cathedral, and the throngs of sightseers out for a Saturday stroll.

Renée looked up at the crisscrossed telephone wires above her head and noticed that dusk had fallen. "We've had quite a bike ride," she said, catching her breath. "May we rest for a minute?"

Propping the tandem bike against a fire hydrant, they sat on the curb. "We'll hail a coach, pile the bike on top, and ride home in style," Steven said, gazing at her with his sparkling emerald-green eyes. He touched her face. "Your cheeks are as red as an apple."

She laughed. "And my hair is blowing every which way."

"It only adds to your charm." He grinned at her. "Can you ride some more? The circus parade will be marching down Broadway. After we watch it, we'll have a cozy dinner for two."

"Oh, yes, I'd love to see the parade. Let's go," she said, feeling refreshed. She mounted the bike again, her feet turning the pedals in unison with Steven.

On Broadway hundreds of torchbearers lit the street as they marched to the beat of drums and the blare of trumpets. Gold-and-red circus wagons, containing lions, tigers, monkeys, seals, and wolves, rumbled by. Next came a military band and acrobats clad in pink tights.

"Look," Steven said, pointing at the Metropolitan Hotel, "there's P. T. Barnum himself."

A white-haired gentleman with a big smile stood on a balcony, waving at everyone below. Renée waved back, straining to get a better view of Mr. Barnum, the owner of such a spectacular circus.

"The parade's almost over," Steven called after a chariot filled with clowns trundled by. "Ready to go?"

"I'm ready," she said, watching the last of the

torches disappearing on Prince Street and heading for Grand Street.

"I'm hungry, aren't you?"

She chuckled. "I could eat one of those elephants that just stomped by." It had been a beautiful day, and it wasn't over yet. She wondered if she would have had such a good time with Nick. Yes, she thought, she knew she would have.

As they bicycled on their two-seater down Broadway, she thought how special Steven was. She loved his easygoing charm and his elegant life-style. After such a pleasant afternoon they'd soon stop and eat at a fancy little café, where they'd talk for hours, and then he'd take her home in a carriage. What bliss. She shook her head, wondering guiltily if she was attracted by the money he spent on her. But studying his shining golden head in front of her, she knew that it was more than wealth. It was Steven, himself!

Chapter
Thirteen

SUNDAY afternoon Renée snuggled in the big chair by the window and opened her diary. As soon as she was comfortable, Blackie jumped into her lap and curled up.

Absentmindedly, Renée stroked his sleek fur and then began to write:

March 11, 1888

Dear Diary,

I'm looking out at a cloudy sky, but it only reminds me how bright and glorious yesterday was. I'm convinced Steven is the one for me. He really cares for me and has shown his love in a hundred ways. The only thing that bothers me is that he wants all my time. And even if he says he doesn't care if I work or not, he doesn't want to share me with a job.

I keep thinking of Nick, too. Mother and Father have been very good about my work at the Gazette and about Steven, but they've shown me in so many subtle ways that my place is with Nick. Even Aunt Olivia, who helped me out of my engagement, seems to prefer Nick. I didn't think she'd side with my parents, but I'm convinced she only wants what's best for me. And if I accept Steven's proposal, I know she'll support my decision.

I have to stop writing and begin work on the hair-fashion article. I have an idea on how to display the various combs and hair ornaments, which I think Flora Blossom will like. I'll hurry to the office right after school.

When Tony came bounding into the room, Renée closed her journal. Tony stood before her, folding his arms. "Wanna play cards?" he asked.

She smiled at him, thinking how tall he was getting. "Sorry, Tony, but I don't have time for card games. I have work to do. Maybe later. All right?"

Tony shrugged, looking wistfully out the window.

"Tony," Olivia said, tying a scarf around her head. "Want to go with me to the park? I'm meeting Mrs. DiLeo. Bring your baseball. Laura will probably be there, and you can play catch."

"Okay," Tony replied enthusiastically, dashing to the closet for his jacket.

"Dress warm," Olivia warned. "It's much colder than yesterday, so wear your muffler and cap."

Tony sighed but wrapped a wool scarf around his neck and put on his black cap. His straight hair lay in fringes on his forehead below the billed cap, and he looked back at Renée, giving her a gap-toothed smile as he went out the door.

When Renée's mother and father came in from a walk, John Conti took off his coat. "Join us for a cup of coffee, Renée."

She hesitated, wanting to start on her layout, but decided that being with her family was more important. Happily, she rose and followed her father into the kitchen. Frank was already sitting at the table, reading the paper. Renée poured him a cup, one for herself, and one for her mother and father.

"So, Renée, what are you working on now?" Mrs. Conti asked with an indulgent smile.

"A hair ornament display."

"Hair ornaments?" John Conti questioned with a quirk of his thick brows. "Such important journalism." But his words were softened with a smile. "And what's the latest style?"

"Ivory combs, tiaras, jet-beaded hairpins, and just all kinds of fancy decorations, like feathers sticking up here." She touched his thick hair, suppressing a laugh.

"I wish I could buy you a diamond tiara," John

said, chuckling. "Wouldn't that be pretty in Renée's black hair, Josie?"

"Very pretty," Mrs. Conti said. "But I don't think you'll be buying her one soon."

"You never know," John boasted. "With spring just around the corner I'll be selling a lot of bicycles." He reached over and pinched his wife's cheek. "And I'll buy you one, too."

"And what will you buy for me?" Frank asked, his dark eyes laughing. "How about a diamond stickpin?"

"Since we're dreaming, why not?" John teased with a short laugh.

Renée sipped her coffee thoughtfully. Steven could buy any of these things and not blink an eye.

Rain began to pelt the windowpanes, and Frank groaned. "I hope it's not like this tomorrow. I've got a twelve-hour shift."

"Let's see the forecast," Renée picked up the *Herald* and turned to the weather, reading aloud: " 'The weather in New York City and vicinity (including points within thirty miles of the city) promises to be generally fair and colder, preceded by partial cloudiness near the coast. Tuesday will be slightly warmer and generally fair.' "

She glanced at Frank. "There. Your day tomorrow sounds fine."

"Not bad," Frank said appreciatively.

"You're working long hours these days," John Conti said with concern.

"Tomorrow is unusual because Al Sloane is sick. But I want the extra hours." The corners of Frank's mouth turned up, meeting his thick mustache. "When Rose and I are married, we'll need furniture." He gulped his coffee and stood up. "Which reminds me. I promised Rose I'd be over by four." He took his jacket off a peg and shrugged into the sleeves. "Don't wait up for me. And you, little sister," he said, touching Renée's nose playfully, "finish your article. One of these days you'll be a famous journalist."

She laughed, grabbing his hand and squeezing. "It's nice to have an older brother who believes in me." Her blue eyes shone warmly.

Suddenly, there was a knock on the door.

"I'll get it," Renée said, jumping up.

Opening the door, she was astonished to see Megan standing in the vestibule and shaking off her rainy cloak.

"Megan!" Renée exclaimed. "What a pleasant surprise!" She took Megan's wet umbrella and opened it. "Let's leave it out here to dry off."

Renée took Megan's stunning red-and-yellow plaid coat and hung it up on the hall tree. Megan's damp curls hung limply around her oval face, but she was smiling as she entered the kitchen. "I hope I'm not intruding," she said, "but Steven and Mother are off to a painting exhibition at the Metropolitan, and it was just too gloomy to stay home alone. I left a note to say I was coming here."

"We love having you," Renée said.

"Yes, we do!" John Conti said pleasantly, scrambling to his feet and offering her a chair. Mrs. Conti reached for the coffeepot, quickly pouring a cup for Megan. "You're always welcome in the Conti home," she said, patting Megan's hand.

Megan chatted easily with Renée's parents until Aunt Olivia and Tony came in around suppertime.

Megan was coaxed into staying for the meal, and when the windowpanes rattled and the rain pounded ferociously, Renée talked her into spending the night. Mrs. Conti jokingly told Olivia that it was her homemade lasagna that convinced Megan to stay.

Tony looked appealingly at his mother. "Can we play a game?" he wheedled.

Mrs. Conti glanced at Renée, nodding imperceptibly.

"Oh, let's do," Megan broke in eagerly.

"All right," Renée said, suddenly grinning at Tony. "What shall we play?" she asked.

"Blowing the Feather," he replied without hesitation.

"Then run and get a bedsheet," Renée ordered, "and we'll begin."

"Blowing the Feather?" Megan asked, a puzzled look on her face.

John Conti pulled the kitchen chairs into a circle. "You'll see, Megan." He indicated a chair and she slipped into it. Renée sat next to her, then Mrs.

Conti, Olivia, and Mr. Conti were seated.

Tony ran forward, handing Olivia the sheet. "Can I be outside the circle?" he asked eagerly, as he flung out his arms.

Renée chuckled. "You'll have to be. There aren't any chairs left."

Olivia methodically unfolded the sheet. "Each one take an edge," she ordered.

"Hold it up to your chin," Renée said to Megan. "Like this."

Smiling, Megan copied everyone in the circle.

Mrs. Conti produced a white feather. "Now," she said to Megan, "Tony will try to catch the feather and the rest of us will try to keep him from getting it. We blow it away from his greedy little hands." She glanced at Tony and smiled.

Megan nodded, her big brown eyes twinkling. "I understand," she said, holding the sheet taut. This will be fun. I wish Charles were here. He loves games!"

Renée thought that Megan's staid fiancé didn't look like the type who enjoyed silly games, but she only nodded and said, "Steven would like it, too."

Megan giggled. "I'll never forget the evening we played Spin the Bottle. Steven and Alicia — " she suddenly stopped, flustered, not daring to look at Renée.

Renée's smile froze on her face. Alicia again! How she hated that name!

Renée's father, oblivious to the reference to Alicia, said cheerfully, "Get ready, Tony!"

The game commenced and Tony tried to grab the feather, but every time he lunged forward, the seated players blew it into the air away from him. Tony's fist came up empty more than once.

One time, however, when the feather floated before Megan, she puffed out her cheeks but blew too late. Tony quickly captured the elusive feather.

"Since the feather was caught in front of you, Megan," Renée explained, "you must take Tony's place."

Tony chortled gleefully as he placed the feather in the middle of the sheet and slid into Megan's chair.

John Conti eyed Megan. "Ready?"

Megan set her feet and thrust out her chin. "Let the feather fly."

The feather flew up in the air, but when Megan reached forward, Renée blew it in Olivia's direction.

After a number of tries, Megan triumphantly caught the feather, tickling Renée under the chin with it. Renée was the next one outside the circle to try to catch the feather.

After they'd finished the game, they each had a glass of apple cider. The raindrops on the roof gave Renée a cozy feeling, and when she caught Megan's eye, she knew Megan felt the same way. She forgot about Alicia, a name out of Steven's past, and just enjoyed being with Megan.

"I'm glad I'm staying overnight," Megan said to

Renée as they undressed for bed. Olivia had offered to sleep on the sofa, so Megan could have her bed.

"So am I," Renée said, looking at Megan warmly. She was really a very sweet girl, and she liked to think Megan was her friend.

"I hear you had a wonderful time biking and seeing the circus parade yesterday," Megan said as a bolt of lightning punctuated her remark. "Steven, I know, had a good time."

"I did, too," Renée said, enjoying any conversation about Steven. Megan could tell her a lot about his likes and dislikes. "Poor Steven at an art show," she said, pouring water into the washbasin. "He would have enjoyed tonight's game."

"He would have," Megan agreed, slipping beneath the covers, "but he had a delightful evening, too. After the exhibition the Tottens were hosting a small dinner party at the Plaza." Megan gave a low laugh. "Steven's never bored."

Renée, scrubbing her face at the washstand, stopped short. Her heart began to beat quickly. Steven was with Alicia, she thought with a dull ache.

Chapter
Fourteen

ON Monday morning when the alarm clock jangled, Renée pulled the covers over her head. Another fifteen minutes of sleep would be delicious, she thought, snuggling deeper beneath the comforter. But she wanted to be at school on time, so she flung off the quilt, yawning and stretching. She glanced out the window, wondering why it was so dark at seven o'clock in the morning. Determinedly she set her bare feet on the cold floor.

Walking gingerly toward the window, she noticed a few cracks in the white mass outside the pane. Snow! Snow that had drifted higher than the window! Was this possible?

She looked over her shoulder at Megan, who was sleeping peacefully. With her blonde hair spread over the pillow, she looked like a golden angel.

Quietly, Renée pulled on her flannel robe and slipped into her felt slippers. Going out, she carefully shut the door. Let Megan sleep as long as she could, she thought. She'd have quite a struggle mushing through the snow to get home.

When Renée entered the kitchen, Aunt Olivia was staring out the back door, shaking her head. "I've never seen so much snow," she muttered.

"Neither have I," answered Renée with a laugh. "It's higher than my bedroom window." She poured milk over her oatmeal and sat down at the table. "It should be fun going to school today."

"There can't be school with all this snow," Olivia said, a worried frown creasing her high forehead. "Plus the thermometer registers ten degrees!"

Renée replied cheerfully, "A little snow isn't going to hurt me." Taking a mouthful of cereal, she went on. "I read the weather forecast yesterday, and nothing was said about snow today. Only that it would be crisp and clear." She glanced around. "Where's Mother?"

"Everyone's gone," Aunt Olivia said, pouring a cup of coffee and joining Renée. "I wish your mother hadn't ventured out to the bakery for bread. She should have stayed here. We could have done our own baking. This would have been a good day for it."

"And Father?"

"He went to work," Olivia said. "Why he did, I

don't know. I doubt if he gets one customer. Who would want to buy a bike in this kind of weather? He left very early, knowing the trains would be crowded and late."

"And is Frank on duty?"

"Yes, and Tony's still sleeping. Since I know he won't be going to school today, there's no reason to wake him."

"Megan's asleep, too. Will she be surprised when she wakes up!"

"I imagine the weatherman was dumbfounded, too. Well," Olivia said with a slight shrug, "he's been wrong before, but this time he really missed the mark!"

After Renée dressed, she kissed Olivia good-bye and went out the door.

She wasn't prepared for the icy blast that greeted her. She tied her scarf over her mouth and nose and set out. Down the slippery street she wended her way. On the north side the sidewalk was completely blocked with snow, but on the south side, where the Contis lived, the sidewalk was passable. The wind blew so hard she couldn't keep her footing, and she grasped the iron railings in front of the apartment houses in order to inch along. One innovative neighbor had propped an ironing board over the steps and slid down that way. Another simply jumped out his second-story window into a snow bank.

On the icy walks Renée lost her balance more

than once, but gritting her teeth she plowed forward. She knew now the schools would be closed. The newspaper office was only six blocks away, but even that seemed impossible.

A horsecar driver turned his mount around, waving off a customer. "It's back to the barn for me and old Dobbin!" he roared against the wind. "Keep your money!"

The man stumbled after the cab, but lost his footing and sprawled in the middle of the street, coattails flying. He tottered upright, shaking his fist at the disappearing cab, then staggered to a coffee shop. That was the last Renée saw of him.

She fought for her breath and stopped to cling to a streetlamp to rest.

When she started out again, she was forced to climb over a downed telephone pole. Next she had to dodge hundreds of ice-coated telegraph, telephone, and electric wires crisscrossing the street like giant strands of a black cobweb.

The Third Avenue elevated train was stopped on its iron trestle high off the ground, and passengers stuck their heads out the window and banged on the sides of the car. Renée could see through the whirling snow that a huge snowbank blocked the tracks. Workmen were out with pails of salt water and brooms to keep the switches thawed, but nothing would move that mountain of snow in front of the engine. The passengers would have a long wait.

Renée forged ahead and finally glimpsed the doorway of the *Gazette*. Never had the doors looked so inviting and welcome.

Fighting the wind that gusted up to seventy-five miles an hour, she tugged and pulled on the closed door, at last managing to pry it open.

Inside, she leaned against the door, breathing hard. What a relief to be away from the biting snow and raging wind.

She removed her boots and scarf and went upstairs to the office. The place was so quiet. Although she heard a clacking typewriter, she saw no one. She hung up her coat and set to work.

Miss Blossom wasn't in, and Renée doubted if she'd be able to make it. That was all right, she thought. She'd finish the layout and have it ready for Miss Blossom's final OK the next day.

Renée didn't know how long she worked, but all at once she noticed the typing had ceased. The silent office caused a tingling in her spine. Where was everyone?

Suddenly a shadow fell across her face. Startled, she looked up.

"Well, look who's here," Mike Webb said, standing in the doorway, hands on hips and chewing a giant cigar. "You should have stayed home!"

"I-I wanted to finish this layout," she said, always intimidated by his scowl.

"Go on home!" he growled. "No one else came in!" He waved his arms. "Here's the biggest storm of the season and I don't have one reporter to cover it!"

"Sir," she said hesitantly, "I'm here. Let me write what happened on the way to work."

"Forget it!" he snapped, looking out the window at the wild snow flurries. "Go home!" he repeated.

"All right," Renée said, daring to add, "but it seems to me that since I'm able to write and I'm the only one around, you'd at least give me a chance."

Mike Webb's frown darkened. "Do you think I'd send a slip of a girl out on an assignment in this?"

Yes, she thought, you would if you thought that slip of a girl could write a story. But Mike Webb didn't trust her to write up a tea party, let alone a newsbreaking story.

Mike Webb glanced at her, his chin thrust out like a bulldog's. "I want you to go home."

Resignedly, she reached for her coat. There was no arguing with Mr. Webb.

His eyes narrowed. "When you get home, write up your impressions and bring them to me in the morning."

"Oh, I will," she said eagerly, smiling with gratitude.

"You understand I'm only letting you do this because there isn't anyone else," he growled. "I don't expect anything, either." Abruptly he turned around and left her, muttering, "It will probably end up in the trash can!"

So he didn't expect anything! Well, she'd show him that she could write! She struggled into her wet boots, tied the scarf around her head, and as she went out the front door, she glanced at the wall clock and noticed it was two o'clock.

The howling wind almost bowled her over, and for an instant she wanted to go back inside. Stubbornly, though, she hung onto the railing, slipping and sliding down the steps.

Returning the way she'd come, Renée reeled against the strong wind, keeping images of falling, sliding, skittering New Yorkers in her mind for her story. Some had formed a line, clinging to one another's shoulders as they fought their way home. All kinds of debris flew by — torn loose signs, awnings, frozen sparrows, derby hats, cardboard boxes, and pieces of glass. Undaunted, Renée skirted a flagpole that had snapped in half and an overturned cart. She was almost hit by a flying umbrella and had to clutch the open door of an abandoned carriage to keep her balance. Catching her breath, she plunged on, often in waist-high drifts.

She passed a policeman rubbing snow on the frost-bitten ears of a newsboy. "Go on home, boy," the policeman said gruffly. "No one needs to read about the weather. They know what's going on."

Renée smiled. It was marvelous to observe people helping each other. And the city was beautiful, too.

The brownstone houses were transformed into glittering snow castles, and the ice had traced lacy designs on windowpanes. The city streets and buildings glittered with a frozen whiteness.

When she went by the elevated train, still stalled from this morning, ladders had been set up. "Twenty-five cents to use my ladder!" a young man hollered. Many riders paid the high fee and clambered down. Raucous singing came from the passengers who elected to remain aboard.

"Want to buy a sandwich, lady?" a young boy asked, carrying a long box. "One dollar each," he called, rushing toward the train.

One dollar, Renée thought, too astonished to respond. Some people were getting rich on this blizzard!

"Want help, little lady?" a policeman shouted at her.

"I'm fine," she called, her words lost in the wind. She gamely plodded forward, crossing the street. A woman had fallen and two men hoisted her to her feet. Between them they dragged her to the curb. Women in high-heeled boots struggled to remain upright. Veils on their hats became so ice-encrusted that they could hardly see. Men's hats blew away.

Renée passed a shoe store just as a salesman placed a sign in the window: ONLY SIZE 13 BOOTS LEFT!

He gave her a big grin as she turned back into

the wind. Evidently, she thought, boot sales were at an all-time high.

As she trudged toward 74th Street, the drifts loomed increasingly higher. Some would eventually reach twenty to thirty feet high. Her breath came raggedly as she staggered through the drifts, twice sinking up to her armpits.

The third time she sank into a snowbank she couldn't extricate herself. A boy on skis offered her a hand and pulled her free. He laughed. "Better find a warm shelter, miss," he said. "I just came from Macy's, and they've set up cots for all the sales-ladies, so they can spend the night."

"I'm almost home," she said in a raspy voice not recognizable as her own. The boy waved and skied away. Another boy, with the wind at his back, whooshed past on snowshoes. How clever they were, she thought. Never had she seen New York-ers like this. Everyone dressed in whatever was warm: outer garments of fur coats, mackinaws, leather jackets, sheepskins, and long overcoats were offset by coonskin hats, Russian cossack hats, bearskin hats, or muskrat caps. One man wore his scarf wrapped around his head like a turban with only his eyes peeking out. He'd wrapped his legs and feet in burlap sacks. Some had tied carpet strips around their legs while others lashed straw wine-bottle covers to their shins. Anything to keep warm, she thought approvingly.

"Hey, there, girlie," a bearded man yelled through blue lips. "Find a warm place." He was short, and his long blue Civil War overcoat dragged in the snow. When his coat flapped open, Renée glimpsed a pair of ragged army leggings. A blast of wind bowled him over, and he dropped on all fours, crawling toward a tavern.

Renée bit her lip. She began to panic as the sky darkened. Was she going in the right direction? She had to get home. She must be near 74th Street by now.

Before her ice-encrusted eyes she saw a policeman take two unconscious girls by their wrists and drag them, like two sacks of potatoes, to a nearby hotel. Renée doggedly went on.

The ferocious gale whipped her scarf around her, and the snow beat against her frozen face like a thousand prickly needles. Suddenly a store window shattered, spraying bits of glass into the air.

"Oh, God," she prayed. Why hadn't she stopped back at the shoe store and revived her chilled body? She staggered and fell but pulled herself back up.

The wind screamed in her ears and the blinding snow blotted out any familiar landmarks. Where was she? Where were the people that had surrounded her before? She was alone. Was she nearing home or was she going in the opposite direction?

A sudden gust blew her like a rag doll into a nearby snowdrift. Weakly she fought to free herself, but she only sank deeper into the snow. Her snow-caked eyelids closed, and she lay back, the soft snow covering her face. She was so numb with cold that she couldn't move. Was this the way her life was to end? she wondered dreamily. She nestled deeper into the snow, yearning to sleep.

Chapter Fifteen

As Renée lay in the snow, she drifted in and out of the most wonderful dream. She had just won a journalism prize for the best story of the year, and Steven had rushed up to give her a sweet congratulatory kiss. Afterward they held hands and strolled in Central Park on a warm moonlit evening. Banks and banks of white roses were everywhere.

All at once Nick confronted them in his white baker's uniform, with a dark scowl on his face. He grabbed her hand, whisking her away from Steven, who grasped her arm. Nick yanked on the other. Suddenly they flung her into a white lilac bush and began to fight. She was horrified and wanted to stop them, but lilac blossoms blanketed her face and she couldn't move.

"Stop," she moaned. "Stop." Her eyes fluttered open, and she feebly moved an arm to brush away the white, cold petals covering her face. Slowly she regained a faraway memory of snow and wind. Then, with startling clarity, she remembered! Panic-stricken, she realized she wasn't in a lilac bush but was engulfed in a ferocious blizzard. She felt the terrifyingly cold snow on her face. She must fight for her life or perish!

"Help!" she called weakly, but in her snow tomb she heard nothing. Her chest felt as if it would burst when she pushed herself into a sitting position, and muscles ached as she struggled to stand. Twice she fell back in the snow.

She fought to free her legs and get away from the snow cocoon that threatened to bury her, but every time she moved a few inches, the snow clung to her like white quicksand, pulling her back. She writhed and wriggled and finally tore loose, shaking off the snow. She took a few ragged breaths through a windpipe that felt as if it were filled with stabbing ice particles. "Help," she whispered again, but the only response was a chill silence.

Tottering forward, she dazedly wondered where she was. Ahead, a glimmer of light shone like a beacon, and she aimed for that.

Reeling and staggering like one of the drunks she'd seen come out of the bars a short time before, she made her painful way toward the wavering light. All at once a powerful hand clamped around her upper arm, and another hand brushed away the powdery snow that clung to her face. "Missy, we're going inside the Men's Club and get you warm."

"Where am I?" she murmured, looking into the red face of a policeman who smiled down at her.

"East Seventy-third Street."

"Thank you, thank you," she whispered. "I'm almost home." She didn't know how close she'd come to never seeing her family again.

"Here we are," he said, opening the door for her. "This is probably the only time you'll get to see the inside of The New York Men's Club."

The room, warm and glowing with small gaslights, smelled of leather. She was so tired her nerves throbbed, and she sprawled in a velvet hall chair.

"Take care of her, will you, Billy?" The policeman said to the bartender. "Give her a hot drink."

"Sure thing," said a slightly built man who wore a long apron and armbands around his striped shirt sleeves.

"Good-bye, missy. You're in good hands now," the policeman said, going toward the door. "Billy's the bartender here, and he'll see that you're thawed out before you set one foot outside again."

Gratefully, she took the cup of steaming tea, but her cold hands trembled and she spilled the liquid on her wrist. But she murmured her thanks and gulped down the hot tea. It seared her throat, but never had a drink tasted better. Little by little, heat returned to her body.

"It's getting dark, miss. Too dangerous for you to be out," Billy said.

"I can find my way now. My home's only a block away."

Her numb toes and fingertips were beginning to tingle. She glanced about at the paneled walls and the plush draperies. Several men sat drinking in tall wing chairs, discussing the storm. Other club members sat at the long teak bar, which faced a sparkling mirror.

Suddenly the door burst open and in staggered a robust, tall man with a large stomach. The frost-coated man collapsed on the rug, and several men ran to his aid. Billy forced whiskey between the man's clenched lips, but the man sputtered and weakly pushed him away. Renée couldn't see the man's face, for it was covered with snow, and icicles dripped from his mustache.

"Roscoe Conkling!" exclaimed one man, who was sitting on a barstool. He jumped off his perch and frantically wiped snow from the newcomer's cheeks, helping to remove his muffler and hat. "What are you doing out in this weather?"

For a while Mr. Conkling's lips moved, but he couldn't utter a sound. His chest heaved and he caught at his neck, loosening his cravat.

When Billy offered him the whiskey again, he drank it down.

"I started out hours ago," he gasped. "I walked all the way from my office on Wall Street." He boastfully stuck out his chest. "It was quite a walk," he said, picking caked snow from his yellow hair and mustache.

Renée remembered that Roscoe Conkling's nickname was "War God of the Norsemen," and that he had a reputation for arrogance. He was an ex-Senator from New York and had had enormous power. He was also quite a ladies' man and had openly pursued a married woman, Kate Sprague. The romance ended when Mr. Sprague chased him with a shotgun. But the real reason he had fallen from power was President Hayes's intense dislike of him.

Roscoe Conkling rose unsteadily to his feet. "I exercise with barbells every day, but this storm was a real test of my strength." He rubbed his red nose. "I took a shortcut across the park at Union Square, where I floundered in a snowdrift for nearly an hour. Fortunately, someone helped me to my feet. For a man of almost sixty, though," he bragged, "I plowed through drifts and made better time than much younger men." Billy offered him a second glass, and he tossed the whiskey down his throat.

Renée knew that Mr. Conkling would be an excellent lead-in for her story on the blizzard. Everyone knew the former New York senator, and she was lucky to have encountered him.

"I went to Superior Court to try the biggest case of my career," Mr. Conkling continued, wheezing and puffing. "Mrs. A. T. Stewart's will is being contested to the tune of eighty million dollars! Would you believe no one showed up? An eighty-milion-dollar lawsuit, and no one came out because of the snow!" His red face became redder. "So I went to my office. Then I came here."

"Couldn't you get a cab?" asked a man from the bar.

Roscoe Conkling paused, fighting for his breath, then replied indignantly, "One of my colleagues offered to share a horsecar, but the driver wanted fifty dollars! The nerve! For fifty dollars I walked the distance!"

Yes, Renée thought, studying the man's florid face, crisscrossed by blue veins, and you almost killed yourself in getting here.

"Sir," she asked, "do you still live up in northern New York State?"

He gave her a stony glance and handed his empty glass to Billy. "Fill her up, again." His glare was disdainful. "Don't you know that no women are allowed in here?"

Billy, the bartender, interceded. "The poor mite was half froze to death. Officer O'Brien brought her in. She could have died."

"Well," Mr. Conkling huffed, "her color looks

good and she's gotten warm. She has a heavy coat and muffler." He pointed to the door. "On your way, miss."

Chagrined, Renée buttoned her coat. She'd get no interview from this boastful man. Now she could understand why President Hayes had disliked him.

Nonetheless, she noted the state he'd been in when he came into the club, and the way he looked, and what he said. Readers would be interested in Roscoe Conkling, and she'd mention him in her article whether he liked it or not.

When she heard the whistling wind, Renée turned up her collar. Even though she had only a block to go, she knew it would be tough-going.

As she was about to leave, a milkman stumbled in, carrying a frozen quart of milk. "I've been out all day," he panted, "and made only six deliveries." He staggered up to the bar and sank down on a stool, holding his head in his hands. "Give me a brandy," he ordered hoarsely. After drinking it, he shook his head. "I'm worried about Peter."

"Peter?" Renée asked with concern. "Is that your son?"

"No, no," he answered. "Peter's my horse. The poor beast has been fighting the snow all day. Once he fell and overturned the wagon. I thought Peter was done for. If he'd broken his leg, I would have had to shoot him. But some lads hoisted up my wagon, and Peter staggered to his feet." He wiped his nose, and tears filled his eyes. "If I can't find him a barn, though, he'll die. His sides are heaving, and he's near cavin' in!"

The bartender whispered a few words to one of the men at the bar.

The man turned and clapped the milkman on the back. "Bring your horse in here, my man. Bring him in."

Startled, the milkman gazed about at the opulent surroundings. "In here?" he asked, unable to believe he'd heard correctly.

"Yes, hurry!" another man urged. "Go and get your horse before he freezes to death."

The milkman slid shakily off his stool and tottered toward the door.

Before long he returned, pulling in a snow-covered horse. The bridle was ice-encrusted and huge clumps of snow surrounded the horse's great, soft eyes.

Renée patted the icy muzzle of the shivering horse and began to break off chunks of snow from his ears and mouth.

"You'll be fine," the short, plump man from the bar said. "You and your horse will both spend the night here."

Renée shook the milkman's hand. "I'm doing an article on the storm. Would you mind if I gave your name?"

"Naw, not at all," the milkman said, as melting snow dripped from his boots onto the lush carpet.

"I'm Aaron Jennings, and don't forget to mention my horse, Peter."

"Oh, I won't," Renée said with a grin, knowing this was the kind of human interest story the readers would like.

She wrapped her scarf up to her eyes and glanced at Roscoe Conkling, who was in a deep, exhausted sleep. Good, she thought. She didn't want to hear any more of his scornful remarks.

Billy, the bartender, waved at her. "Take care, miss, and don't get blown into another snowdrift."

" 'Bye, Billy," she said, her voice sounding muffled by her scarf. "And thanks."

As she opened the door, she hoped the wind had died down, but an icy blast sent her reeling backward. If anything, the wind was stronger than ever.

She headed into the frigid wind, floundering in and out of drifts, the snow cutting against her face like slivers of fine glass.

At last she saw the street sign indicating 74th Street, and a ragged sob of sheer relief tore from her throat. "Thank you, Lord," she said out loud.

In the wavering light of a street lamp she saw an arm sticking out of a snowbank. She struggled forward. When she drew near, her heart leaped in her throat. The plaid coat sleeve was Megan's!

Chapter Sixteen

RENÉE waded into the drift and scrambled toward Megan, who was buried in the snow. Frantically she dug to uncover her friend, scooping away the snow. "Megan! Megan!" she shouted. "Can you hear me?"

But Megan's eyes were closed, her pale face waxen and her blue lips sealed.

Renée's cold breath turned to ice in her throat. "Megan," she moaned. "Wake up, wake up!" She shook Megan. Was she dead? How long had her friend lain here?

Panic-stricken, she seized Megan's shoulders, shaking her back and forth like a limp cloth doll.

Megan's arm moved, and a soft moan escaped her

stiff, frozen lips. "R-Renée?" she asked piteously. "Is it really you?"

"Megan!" Renée cried. "You're alive!" Clasping Megan to her breast, she joyfully rocked her to and fro.

Then, picking up a handful of snow, she briskly rubbed it over Megan's cheeks to revive her circulation. Megan whimpered in protest.

But when Renée tried to lift her, Megan fell back again, a dead weight. Renée knew it was critical to get Megan out of the Arctic-like cold and into a warm shelter. And soon. Or they'd both perish.

Megan's eyes flickered halfway open, then shut again. "Don't sleep," Renée warned her hysterically. "Stay awake, Megan. Oh, please, open your eyes again!"

But Megan's head lolled back into the snow, and she didn't move. Renée grabbed her arm and tugged with every ounce of strength she had left. Little by little she pulled Megan out of the drift, and once in the clear, jarred her awake by slapping her face. One, two, three times! Megan lifted an arm feebly to ward off the blows, but Renée stubbornly shook her. "On your feet!" she commanded, battling a resistant Megan. At last she got her to stand, but as soon as Megan was upright, she slipped back down into the snow.

"Let me sleep," she murmured.

"Get up!" Renée shouted, yanking Megan forward and forcing the semi-conscious girl onto her feet. She threw Megan's arm about her shoulder and started out. Swaying, they trudged down the narrow path, mounds of snow on either side. Home should be just a few more yards, but the fury of the raging wind was more than Renée could stand. She felt she couldn't go another step. Suddenly her scarf tore free, flying away, high on the wind. Helplessly, she watched the muffler flutter forlornly as it caught on a telephone wire.

Holding up her mittened hand to protect her nose and mouth, Renée determinedly propped up Megan, who grew heavier by the minute. Step by step she plodded ahead, remembering how easily Officer O'Brien had half carried her to the men's club. If only the brawny policeman would appear to help her again! Home was only a short distance, she kept reminding herself, as she faltered under the buffeting winds and Megan's weight.

She sank to her knees, each painful breath like a cutting blade against her throat. Would she have to give up? No, she firmly told herself. Never! But her body wouldn't go on. She'd reached the end of her endurance. She choked back a sob, her eyes glazing over. What little strength she had in reserve vanished. Suddenly her knees buckled, and she collapsed. Spread-eagled in the snow, Renée gave way to a heavenly rest. Megan, happy to be left alone, curled into a ball and slept.

Renée stirred, fighting to open her eyes. She realized that sleep would be deadly and that she dare not linger there. Dragging herself upright, she took a few rocky steps, the freezing snow beating against her numb face. Her eyelids were heavy with frost, and she could barely see.

How far away from home was she? Would she ever see her family again? If only she'd been more affectionate and caring. Oh, if she could feel her father's strong arms around her in a bear hug; or see her mother's blue eyes soften when she gazed at her; or hear Aunt Olivia sing a gentle Italian lullaby. Tears froze on her lashes at the memories. If she could only touch Tony's darling face once more or nuzzle Frank's neck and smell the lemon scent he wore. And would she ever feel Steven's lips pressed to hers or warm to Nick's happy grin? And Blackie. How she'd love to cuddle her cat and hear his purr of contentment. Her throat ached with a terrible yearning. Then, with a stubborn despair, she plunged on, not knowing if she was headed in the right direction.

Not having the stamina to get Megan on her feet again, Renée grabbed her wrist and tried to drag her like a sack of flour. But it was no use. She couldn't budge her.

When Megan moaned, Renée halted, letting loose of her arm. "Stand up," she coaxed, gently patting Megan's cheeks. She attempted to lift her once more. "Only a short distance and we'll be warm." But even as she spoke the words, she wondered if they'd ever feel heat and vitality again. How could they ever make it? Maybe if she went on alone, Renée reasoned, she could bring back help. But even as the thought crossed her mind, she rejected it. She'd never leave Megan. Yet she couldn't carry her, either. No longer was she able to fight against the savage wind. The blizzard had won! Some spark within her, though, wouldn't let her quit. Again she tried to lift Megan.

This time Megan responded, stumbling to her feet. With her red-and-yellow plaid coat covered with packed snow, she clung to Renée. "Where am I?" she said in a voice so weak that Renée could barely make out the words.

"We're close to home," Renée answered reassuringly.

"Mother and Steven," Megan stopped, groping for words, "will be glad to see me."

"No," Renée corrected, "we're near *my* home." But Megan didn't seem to hear. She allowed herself to be guided along, setting one foot in front of another. At least, Renée thought, she no longer had to drag her.

A sleigh went gliding by, pulled by four horses. Renée flung out her hands. "Stop!" she yelled, but her voice was only a croak in the storm's roar. She watched hopelessly as the sleigh disappeared in a cloud of snow.

Abruptly, a gust of wind whirled the two girls around. Renée was blown off her feet. Megan screamed, and the sound unleashed a final spurt of energy within Renée. Weakly, she rose, staring into the dark, trying to get her bearings. Was she still going the right way? All she could see were banks of snow and blowing ice crystals.

Megan tugged at her sleeve. "Where are we?"

Suddenly, through a burst of swirling snow, Renée glimpsed her apartment. "We're home!" she cried jubilantly.

Relentlessly, she pulled Megan up the steps. Both girls stumbled and fell. At last they reached the front door, and Renée pounded on it. No one answered. With the last bit of waning strength, she banged a second time. But who could hear her against the howling wind? She dropped to the stoop, clawing at the door. Megan collapsed beside her.

Fiercely fighting against the tide of exhaustion that washed over her aching body, Renée got to her knees. Even though her strength was drained, she wouldn't give up! How ironic it would be to freeze to death on her own front steps! Crawling to the doorbell, she pulled herself up and frantically pressed it. Didn't they hear? Oh, please, answer me, she prayed. Please, before it's too late!

She slumped forward, falling across Megan.

Chapter
Seventeen

ALL at once, the door flew open, and a shaft of light fell across Renée's face. She weakly lifted her head but couldn't see who had answered because her eyelashes were coated with frozen snow. Feebly, she held out her hand and felt welcome, strong arms drag her across the threshold.

When the door slammed shut, blotting out the storm's constant roar, she knew she was safe!

Dimly, Renée heard Aunt Olivia say, "Let me get their coats off."

"I'll help," Mrs. Conti said urgently. "Tony, you bring brandy and blankets and heap more coal on the fire."

"R-Renée," he babbled. "Is she all right?"

"She'll be fine," Mrs. Conti answered comfortingly. "Now, scoot."

"My little girl," John Conti said, cradling Renée's head close to his barrel chest.

"Time for that later, John," Olivia said firmly. "Carry the girls into the bedroom. Josephine and I will take off their wet clothes and get them into flannel nightgowns and robes."

After John had laid them on the bed, his sister gently shoved him out the door. "Go and help Tony."

Renée gratefully opened her eyes and tried to help her aunt unfasten the buttons on her dress, but her numb fingers were too stiff and frozen. Olivia removed Renée's hand. "I'll unbutton it," she said, quickly undoing the dress and stripping it off.

Renée relished the warmth, safety, and love she felt surrounding her.

Dressed in warm nightgowns and robes, both girls were seated before the stove, and John forced brandy down their throats.

Renée sputtered and coughed, but the fiery liquid coursed through her body, down to her toes, warming her. When she handed the glass back to her father, she impulsively grabbed his wrist and kissed it. "I love you," she choked.

"Shhh," John said, but tears glistened in his eyes. "Rest, my darling."

Megan shivered even though a quilt was wrapped around her. "I-I don't think I'll ever get warm," she said, gratefully taking the coffee that Aunt Olivia offered her.

Renée warmed her hands by putting them around her hot coffee cup. Feeling her mother's arms about her neck, she began to cry. "I don't know what's wrong with me," she apologized softly. "It's so wonderful being with everyone I love again." She rested her hand on Tony, who was sitting cross-legged beside her chair. "Where's Frank?" she asked, worry lines furrowing her forehead.

"On duty," her father responded. "He'll be sleeping at the station until the crisis is over."

"What happened to you?" Mrs. Conti asked, pulling up a chair.

"It's a long story," Renée answered, a small smile flickering across her face when Blackie arched his back against her leg. She picked up her cat, remembering her thoughts during the storm. She thought she'd never see this moment.

"All I remember is that Renée saved my life!" Megan said promptly. Her blonde hair was matted around her flushed face, and a damp strand fell into her eyes. Mrs. Conti leaned forward and brushed it back from her face.

"But you left for home right after lunch, Megan," Olivia said, shaking her head in disbelief. "You mean you've been out in the storm since one o'clock?"

Megan nodded, pulling her patchwork quilt closer around her. "I tried to walk, but the fury of the wind was too much for me. It took me over an hour to go one block, and I couldn't stay on my feet. I don't know how many times I fell. The last time I got to my feet I was spun around like a top and tossed into a snowdrift. I struggled and struggled, calling for help, but no one heard me. And the more I fought to get free, the deeper I sank." She gazed at Renée. "If it hadn't been for you, I'd have died." Suddenly she chuckled, touching her face. "My cheeks still burn from your slaps!"

"Sorry," Renée murmured with a grin.

"It's a good thing you were burrowed in a snowbank," John Conti said. "It probably saved your life — kept you out of the wind." His eyes grew grave. "But you couldn't have survived many more hours." His gaze shifted from Megan to Renée, as if he had to convince himself that they were really alive. "Josephine," he said suddenly, jumping up, "is there any minestrone soup left?"

"A whole potful," she answered, following him into the kitchen. "That's what the girls need. Soup and sleep."

"Lots of sleep," Renée called after her. Her body ached, and she was so exhausted she could scarcely hold her head up. She and Megan exchanged weary, understanding glances.

"I'm going to sleep for a week," Megan said, with only her tired eyes peeking out from the blanket.

"Me, too," Renée echoed. Then she remembered the article she was to write about the blizzard. Well, in the morning she'd describe the people she'd met, the ferocity of the storm, and the way she felt when she knew she was going to die. By tomorrow the storm should be over. But when she stared out the window at the blowing snow and listened to the furious howling wind, she wasn't so certain.

While eating the rich Italian vegetable soup, Tony handed Renée and Megan each a slice of bread. He had a huge grin on his face.

"What have you been up to?" Renée asked, knowing that impish look of his only too well.

"I made fifty dollars today," he said proudly.

Renée's eyes widened as she stopped eating. "Fifty dollars!" she repeated. "How?"

"Well," he said slowly, savoring his triumph, "I pulled my sled over to DiLeo's Bakery to see if Mama needed help. On the way over, Mrs. Michelini asked if I'd bring back a loaf of bread. Then Mrs. Genovese stuck her head out the window and wanted a dozen rolls, and Mrs. Francone ran out and asked for a cake." He laughed with glee. "It went on like that all morning."

"I bundled him up good," Aunt Olivia said. "He had on three pair of pants and two sweaters, plus his mackinaw and a black scarf around his eyes." She chuckled. "He looked like a roly-poly raccoon."

"I bet I made twenty trips," Tony said excitedly. "And every time I brought more bakery goods, the women not only paid me but gave me a big tip!"

"Tony," Renée said with a smile, chucking him

under his chin, "leave it to you to be quite the little businessman. What are you going to do with all your money?"

"Buy a new Safety bicycle," he said promptly, glancing at his father. "I know Papa will give me a good price."

Mr. Conti lightly grabbed Tony's shoulder, squeezing it. "You bet I will," he promised.

Renée's eyes drooped and her head nodded.

"Renée," Megan said, "let's go to bed."

Renée jerked awake and stood up, her legs still rubbery and unsure. "Good-night, everyone," she said softly as she took Megan's hand.

"I'll tuck you both in," Mrs. Conti said, putting her arm around Renée's waist.

That night Renée slept soundly. Once she thought she'd heard a pounding on the door, but she drifted back into a deep sleep.

Tuesday morning she awoke refreshed but was disappointed to see the snow still swirling outside. Getting dressed, she groaned, feeling a grinding pain in every muscle. But she moved quickly into the living room to her father's desk. She had an article to write!

Lifting open the rolltop, she took paper and pencil and began to write. She could hear her mother and Olivia in the kitchen, but she didn't want to stop, even for a cup of coffee.

Furiously, she scribbled all morning, reliving the adventure of the day's storm. She wrote, crossed out, and rewrote until she had a legible copy for Mr. Webb. She was pleased with the impressions of her ordeal that she'd set down — her meeting with the Honorable Mr. Roscoe Conkling and her life-and-death struggle getting home with Megan. It was an exciting story, and she thought she'd told it well. Now, she thought, if only Mr. Webb liked it.

When she sat down to eat, Aunt Olivia's sad face alarmed her. "Has something happened to Frank? Where's Mother?"

"Josephine's gone over to the Woods' place, and nothing's happened to Frank," Olivia answered, the lines in her face deepening. "It's the Wood boys, who live on Seventy-third Street." She shook her head, retreating to the stove to stir a bubbling sauce.

Renée remembered Carl and Teddy Wood. "What happened?" she asked quietly, sensing bad news.

"They were found early this morning in a drift. They had gone to pick up their newspapers." She dabbed at her eyes with the corner of her apron. "Carl was nine and Teddy only seven."

"Oh, no," Renée whispered. "How awful." She felt sick inside, wondering how she could comfort the Wood family. How many more tragedies like that had happened the day before? She wondered, not knowing then that the storm which raged from Maryland to Maine would take four hundred lives.

"Mr. Wood knocked on our door last night, asking if we'd seen his boys."

So that was the pounding I'd vaguely heard in my sleep, Renée thought. She rose and put her arms around Aunt Olivia. For an instant they stood locked in each other's arms. Then Renée said quietly, "I've got to go to work."

"Take care," Olivia said, patting her hand. "The thermometer registers zero, so dress warmly."

With a heavy heart Renée set out, thinking of the two young boys who had lost their lives in the blizzard. She hoped Mrs. Morison realized that Megan was safe. Otherwise she'd be worried sick. She'd known Megan planned to visit them, but she'd be relieved to hear her daughter was asleep at the Conti apartment!

The six blocks to the *Gazette* were very rough-going. The wind had died down somewhat, but every once in a while, strong gusts blew across the street and drifts piled high. Everywhere lines were down, and debris littered the white blanket of snow. In the distance she saw an elevated engine dangling over the side, and the trains behind piled in a heap.

Hundreds of workers were shoveling snow from the streets, trying to make a dent in the sixteen inches of snow that had fallen the day before and that was still falling. Renée stepped along briskly in the newly cleared sidewalk path. She noticed that some workers wielded a pickax to chop free the ice.

As she passed one apartment, a mailman stopped and yelled up at the upper window covered by snow, "Any Miller or Johnson at home? Come down and get your mail or lower a basket!"

"Good morning," Renée said.

"Morning, miss," the mailman answered. "Cold and snowy enough for you?"

"More than enough," she answered with a laugh and hurried past.

Going on, she noticed a sign planted in a snow-bank: THIS WAY TO THE KLONDIKE! At least the people's sense of humor was coming out.

She reached the newspaper office and hurried to tell Mrs. Morison that Megan was safe. When she entered the office, Mr. Webb, seated across from Mrs. Morison, was saying, "The blizzard special edition will be out by four this afternoon."

"Good," she answered, then glancing up she saw Renée. She leaped up and ran to her. "Is Megan all right?"

"Megan is fine," Renée said. "She's at my house."

"Thank God," Mrs. Morison said, sighing in relief. "Since you have no phone, there was no way I could find out."

"But we had quite an adventure, which I wrote about. It's all here." From her pocket she pulled out her folded article, offering it to Mr. Webb.

But he didn't notice her outstretched hand. Her heart sank. Didn't he remember telling her to write about the storm?

He laughed, turning back to Mrs. Morison. "I had quite an adventure myself coming to work." He paused to light his cigar. "I walked across the East River on an ice floe," he said, blowing a puff of blue smoke into the air.

"You what?" Mrs. Morison asked incredulously.

"That's right. A mass of ice jammed between Brooklyn and Manhattan, and hundreds of people simply slid their way to the other side. Never seen anything like it in my life! A couple of thousand must have gotten across. Tugboats were sent in to break up the ice pack, and you've never heard such a grating, grinding roar in your life! A few men were stranded on islands of ice. When the ice broke into small pieces, they had to leap from one chunk to another to keep from falling off. Finally a tug came along and rescued them."

"Unbelievable!" Mrs. Morison said. "Whoever heard of being able to cross the East River on frozen ice? I think you should write up your account, Mr. Webb."

"Maybe I will," he said with a chuckle, rising. "At any rate, I've got a paper to get out." As he turned to leave, Renée approached him.

"Mr. Webb," she said tentatively, "this is the story I wrote." Again she handed him her article.

Mr. Webb lifted his shaggy eyebrows and looked with astonishment from Renée to the paper. With a disdainful snort he finally took the article and stuffed it into his back pocket. "I'll bet this is a prizewinner," he muttered, winking at Mrs. Morison.

"I think it's good," Renée stated positively, but a quick and disturbing thought assailed her. She wondered if Mr. Webb would even bother to read it.

Chapter Eighteen

GRIMLY, Renée watched Mr. Webb's retreating back. If he'd only known what she'd gone through in the storm. But the way in which he'd contemptuously stuffed her blizzard article into his back pocket showed he had no intention of reading it. Her description of the storm, the people she'd met, and the death struggle of her and Megan meant nothing to him.

"Don't mind Mike Webb," Zena Morison said with a wry smile, noting the dismay on Renée's face. "Even if he dislikes a person, if the writing is good, he'll print it."

I doubt that, Renée thought bitterly, feeling a hollowness inside. How could she ever become a journalist if she couldn't even get her stories read?

"Come, Renée," Zena said, leaning back in her swivel chair, "sit down and tell me what happened to you and Megan yesterday." Her bright green suit and flyaway red hair were in stark contrast to the dull surroundings of the wooden desk, worn leather chair, and black file cabinets.

Renée launched into the retelling of her battle with the wind and blinding snow. When she told about discovering Megan in a snowbank, Zena bent forward anxiously.

"And so," Renée concluded, "after a good night's sleep, I'm as good as new. And Megan will be, too," she said with a grin, "once she wakes up."

"I was frantic about her, naturally," Zena said, "but when Frank phoned me from the police station late Sunday night, I knew Megan would have the good sense to stay Monday, too. I never dreamed she'd foolishly start out." Her brilliant hazel eyes warmed as she gazed at Renée. "You saved my daughter's life and almost lost your own in the attempt."

Modestly, Renée stared at her hands clasped in her lap. "I-I was just glad I spotted Megan," she said, smiling at Mrs. Morison. "We've become good friends." And they had, too. Megan had been warm and friendly these past few days. Like a sister.

"I know," Zena said, "that Megan has a knack of sometimes choosing the wrong friends, but in you, she's really chosen a winner."

"Thank you," Renée said simply. She then added

softly, "You must be so proud of both Megan and Steven."

"Yes, I am lucky to be blessed with such nice children, although at times, Megan can be trying." She paused. "But she's learning. She's learning."

Renée's eyes focused on the picture of Grover Cleveland hanging on the wall behind Mrs. Morison's desk. She wondered if Megan liked her for herself or because she was fascinated with Renée's kind of life, which was so different from her own. If Megan had to choose between her and Alicia, she was certain Alicia would be the one she'd select. Megan was a puzzle at times, and Renée had no idea how she'd react if she and Steven became engaged. Well, she couldn't worry about Megan. She had her own concerns. She was fighting to become a reporter, and Mr. Webb was doing everything he could to prevent it.

Zena Morison stood up, her thin figure looking trim and neat in her tailored suit. "Steven and I played a lot of checkers during the storm. I'm sure he would have much preferred your company. He talked about you incessantly." A tiny smile played about her lips. "I do believe my son's finally fallen in love."

Renée blushed. "I was wondering how he got along yesterday," she said softly.

"I'm sure you were," Zena said, a glint of amusement in her eyes. "Well, I must be going," she said. "Today I'm interviewing Mark Twain, who's staying at the Murray Hill Hotel." She chuckled, flinging her green fur-trimmed coat about her shoulders. "I know he's fit to be tied, because of the storm. He's been holed up for two whole days, expecting his wife, Olivia, to join him. But if she's as smart as I think she is, she'll have stayed in Connecticut." She jabbed a long ruby pin into her broad-brimmed hat and picked up her satchel. "I can't wait to get his views on the blizzard."

All at once Mr. Webb, shirt sleeves rolled up to the elbow and vest unbuttoned, reappeared in the doorway. "I'm running your story, Renée Conti," he said abruptly.

"Y-you're what?" she stammered, starring wide-eyed at the pudgy man before her.

"I *said*," he repeated, "that I'm running your story on the front page!"

"On the front page?" Renée echoed stupefied.

"Are you deaf, Miss Conti?" he shouted. "Yes, on the front page. You wrote a darn good story!"

For a moment Renée said nothing, then a smile spread over her face. "Oh, Mr. Webb, you don't know how happy you've made me."

"I'm not interested in making you happy," he growled, "but I am interested in seeing more of your stories."

"You mean real stories?" she said calmly, all the while wanting to give a wild whoop.

"Real stories. No more teas and weddings." He pulled out his watch from his vest pocket. "You'll be assigned to Frederick Bromley." He gave her a glowering glance. "When school's out, that is."

Frederick Bromley! she thought. One of the top reporters on the staff. Impulsively she grabbed Mr. Webb's hand and shook it. "Thank you, Mr. Webb. Thank you a million times."

"Now don't think that because you've written *one* good front-page story that you'll get plum assignments," he said gruffly. "I expect hard work and then we'll see. Maybe this was a one-time story!"

But Renée wasn't bothered by Mr. Webb's opinion. She knew she had lots more good stories inside. She was so happy she didn't know whether to laugh or cry.

"Now, Mike," Mrs. Morison intervened. "I'm certain Renée will give you other good articles. And you've shown perception in giving her a chance." She turned to Renée. "Congratulations, my dear, on your first major published story." With these words she went out the door, looking very pleased with both Renée and Mr. Webb.

After Mr. Webb left, Renée, smiling to herself, fell back in her chair, and contemplated her story on the front page. Oh, it was too wonderful to be true. But, she reminded herself, she got her break because she was the only reporter there yesterday. No wonder Mr. Webb asked her to write about the storm. But she didn't care how her opportunity had come about, she thought blissfully. She only knew she was on her way to becoming a journalist! She hadn't been this happy since, well, since Steven had asked her to marry him. She touched the gold heart at her throat, thinking of her golden-haired beau and wondering when she'd be seeing him. Now, however, she had newspaper work on her mind and dared not think of Steven.

Her steps were springy as she went into Miss Blossom's office and pulled out the hair display sheet, viewing the fancy ornaments. She couldn't help thinking how ordinary this display seemed compared to her account of the blizzard.

When Miss Blossom swirled in, her plump cheeks as red as cherries, and her coat covered with snow, she said, "Oh, my, it's frigid out today. My feet are like blocks of ice." She removed her scarf and draped it over her chair. "Yesterday I wasn't able to get out my front door because drifts had piled up to the second story and not a soul in sight to shovel." Hanging her coat on a peg, she faced Renée, smiling. "Did you get into the office yesterday?"

"Yes, I did," she answered. "I only live six blocks away, but trying to get here felt more like ten miles!"

Flora Blossom, rubbing her hands together, looked over Renée's shoulder at the hair display, nodding her approval.

The afternoon went quickly as Renée helped Miss Blossom with a new spring fashion layout. Right now, the pretty spring dresses and hats seemed ridiculous when there was heavy snow and ice massed outside the window.

As Renée bundled up to leave, Steven came dashing in. "Renée!" he said, taking off his muskrat hat and slapping it against his boots, causing snow to fly. "I'm glad to see you. When Mother came home and told me you were here, I rushed over. You're a cheerful sight in your red dress." He pulled her forward.

She thought contentedly, This is where I belong. How refreshing his cold, frosty overcoat felt against her warm cheek.

"I'm so proud of you, Renée," he whispered against her hair.

Renée snuggled closer, pleased that he'd heard about her article. "Mr. Webb's printing it on the front page," she murmured.

He pulled back, his blond brows slanting upward, and stared blankly at her. "What are you talking about?" Puzzled, he pushed back an unruly wave of hair that fell into his eyes. "Oh," he laughed, suddenly understanding. "I didn't mean your little article, I meant your rescue of Megan."

"Oh," she said, disappointed that he didn't seem interested in her blizzard article.

He took her hand. "I've a carriage, a driver, and four horses waiting. On the way home, you can tell me how you got Megan out of the snowbank."

"You'll read all the details in tomorrow's edition," she said smugly, lifting her head, and walking with him out the door and into the numbing cold.

A twinkle lit his green eyes. "I know you're pleased about your front-page story and if you're pleased, then I'm happy, too." He helped her into the carriage and climbed in after her, then gave a sharp rap on the roof. The driver cracked his whip, and the horses started off through the snow at a brisk pace. "You know," he said teasingly, "neither you nor Megan should have been out in the storm."

"But I *was* out in it," she responded with annoyance, surveying the mounds of snow on either side of the street, on top of which three more inches would be added that day. "I was lucky that Mr. Webb read my write-up and liked it." She faced him, unable to suppress her shining smile. "Oh, Steven," she said excitedly, "just wait until you read it. It's such a good article!"

"I'm sure it's an excellent article, darling." Steven laughed, putting his arm around her and pulling her near. "But I almost lost you in a blizzard. Your life is more important to me than any old story."

Although she stayed in his arms, the animation had left her face.

"You're safe now and in my arms," he said, gently pressing her closer. "Let's not even think of the *Gazette*. Think of me."

Suddenly the elation she'd felt at having her first major story published evaporated. Why wasn't Steven excited for her? she thought, feeling a squeezing hurt around her heart.

Chapter
Nineteen

ON the way home from the newspaper, Renée nestled beside Steven in the carriage. As they passed the elevated platform, she noticed two snowplows clearing the tracks. And everywhere she looked, an army of shovelers were piling up snow as they cleared streets and sidewalks.

It was the day after the storm, and she was not only exhausted, but when she contemplated the many lives that had been lost, she was sad as well. Even though the biting cold remained, at least the punishing wind had died down. Snow continued to fall, but the whirling wind was no longer of blizzard proportions.

Arriving home, Steven saw her to the door. "Sorry, I can't come in," he said, "but I'm expected back at the office in thirty minutes." He took her hand, gazing into her eyes. "Will I see you tomorrow night?"

His eyes were so appealing that she tried to forget his uncaring attitude when she'd told him about her front-page story. She smiled and said, "I'd love to go out."

"We'll go to Carlo's and have dinner. Is seven okay?"

"Seven is perfect," she murmured, lifting her lips to his. She no longer remembered how upset she'd been.

Going into the hall, she removed her coat, hat, and galoshes, thinking about Steven. She knew he loved her, but increasingly she felt his love was rather selfish. Her time and attention belonged to him, and during whatever hours were left she could play at journalism. Well, she thought with a secretive smile, she'd just have to train him differently. She had priorities, too. And her first was to be a newspaperwoman!

When she entered the living room, she was delighted to see the family seated around Frank, who was sprawled out in a chair with his feet propped on a footstool.

"Hi, Renée, join us," he called. Lines of fatigue etched his round face, and his eyes were ringed with dark circles. Even his mustache drooped. "I just got home," he said, resting his head on the chair pillow.

"Frank!" she cried, running to him. She wrapped her arms around his neck and gave him a kiss. "Are you all right?" She eyed his wrinkled uniform, caked with dirt. "Here," she said, unbuttoning one of the double rows of brass buttons. "Let me unbutton your jacket."

He laughed in a deep, jovial way. "I'm fine, just dead tired after working two double shifts." His rugged face looked even more rough-hewn, his cheeks and forehead were wind-whipped red, and he needed a shave. "I'm not the only one, though. Every policeman was placed on a twenty-four-hour alert, and all time off was canceled. It's interesting, however, there's been no looting, and arrests for stealing have been less than on most days."

Renée sat on the footstool's edge, unlacing Frank's boots.

"Renée," her father explained, "Frank was telling us about his post during the storm."

Her eyes grew big. "And where were you stationed?" she asked breathlessly.

"On the Brooklyn Bridge," Frank answered. "The authorities didn't reopen it until today. What a sight." Frank heaved a deep sigh. "That bridge swayed back and forth like a hammock."

"Did people try to cross it?" Olivia asked, putting down a lace collar she was tatting.

"In droves," Frank replied. "We had to use our billy clubs to keep them back. After all, that bridge is the only way into Manhattan from Brooklyn. The cable cars stopped running Monday noon, their bearing wheels frozen stiff."

"What did you do?" Renée asked, picturing her brother in the relentless wind and snow as he tried to keep pedestrians from risking their lives.

"Well, my job was to keep people off the bridge's pedestrian path." Frank shook his head, running his hand through his disheveled hair. "Before the police patrol was assigned to shut it off, you never saw so many fools swarm onto the bridge. You'd have thought they were giving away dollar bills on the other side. Bowler hats by the hundreds sailed out over the river as men clutched the icy railings and dragged their way across, hand over hand. They had to inch their way, high in the air, with the East River below." His mouth set in a grim line. "I dashed after one small lad who was blown over the side. Poor tyke. He yelled at the top of his lungs but managed to cling to the bridge's cable until I could grab him and pull him to safety."

"No one fell into the river, did they?" Mrs. Conti asked anxiously, handing Frank a cup of cappuccino.

"No, no," he said quickly, accepting the hot coffee, "but once our precinct captain decided to shut the bridge down, we had to fight to keep a few from crossing. The weight of the snow on the bridge, plus the people, could have sent everything plunging into the water."

"That was a real test of the Brooklyn Bridge, eh, Frank?" asked John Conti.

"Right. It's only been five years since it was dedicated, so the storm surely proved its strength." He paused, sipping the hot coffee. "If it could withstand yesterday's gale, it can stand up to anything. When the bridge reopened this morning, thousands of people streamed across."

"Oh, Frank," Renée said, laying her head on his knee. "You weren't out in the storm the whole time, were you?"

"No," he chuckled. "No man could have survived all day and all night, too. The police set up a rest station where we could get a hot meal and sleep for an hour or two." His tired eyes lit up. "One good thing came out of the storm, though," he said with a wide smile.

"What?" Tony asked as he came in from the kitchen, chewing on an apple.

"Well," Frank said proudly, "I got a promotion."

"That's my son," John Conti said. "What's your new job?"

"I'm assigned to the Broadway Squad, which patrols from Bowling Green to Forty-second Street. Only sixty-four officers are attached to this squad, and it's considered the most elite in the city. I was lucky to be chosen," he said. "One of my main jobs will be to answer tourist questions."

"That doesn't sound very dangerous," Tony said.

"The only danger will be directing heavy traffic. Hackney cabs, delivery carts, and carriages jam Broadway." He rose, stretching. "I'll be issued a new uniform, too. The men on the Broadway Squad are famous for their sharp, natty appearance."

"You'll be quite the dandy," Renée teased, but she was happy for her brother. After all, he was only twenty, and already he'd received a promotion. "I hope you get a raise."

"Ten dollars a month," he boasted, "and my hours are from 7 A.M. to 6:30. Now Rose and I can buy that sofa she saw in Macy's window." He yawned. "I'm going to bed and," he said, giving both Olivia and his mother a warning glance, "don't wake me in the morning. I have tomorrow off and I plan to sleep all day."

"What about supper, Frank?" Mrs. Conti said with concern. "You must be starved. I'm roasting a chicken, and your aunt made ravioli."

"Too tired," he said. "I'll just have a glass of milk."

"No milk," Tony piped up. "I've been to Dunston's Grocery twice today, and they haven't had any deliveries since the storm."

"The city is hard-hit," John said. "No milk. No meat. No foodstuffs. Luckily," he stopped, smiling at his wife, "Josie has kept our pantry well stocked."

"I saw Sam DiLeo today," Mrs. Conti said, "and his bakery was cleaned out by noon yesterday. He's trying to get more flour. Nick went out this afternoon to find some so they can start baking again."

"How is Nick?" Renée asked softly.

"The boy's doing well," her father answered, gazing at her. "When they open their bakery on Second Avenue, he'll make a success of it. Nick's a bright boy." A tiny smile hovered about his lips.

Renée smiled back. Her father, always the optimist, was still hoping that she and Nick would get together. She hated to disappoint him, but by now he should realize that her future was with Steven.

As Frank headed for the bedroom, Tony ran up to him. "I shoveled Mrs. Michelini's walk today, and she paid me twenty-five cents an hour."

"Good for you, Tony," Frank said. "Do you know that's what the city's paying grown-up men to shovel?"

"Honest?" Tony asked. His eyes were sparkling as he looked adoringly at his older brother.

"Uh-huh," Frank said, stretching again. "Twenty-five cents an hour, and they've hired 17,000 shovelers."

"Wow!" Tony exclaimed. "Tomorrow I'm going out and shovel again. I've already made fifty dollars on deliveries!"

"Are the schools still closed?" John asked, frowning.

Tony nodded vigorously. "All week," he said with a happy grin.

"Good-night, everyone," Frank said with a smile, going to bed.

After supper Renée soon followed. Her legs and

arms ached from Monday's struggle, and she was still exhausted.

On Wednesday morning on the way to the *Gazette*, Renée walked between huge snowbanks. The wind was cutting, and snow was falling again, but the day was warmer and she moved with a lively step. Everywhere men were cleaning the walks, and she heard metal scraping on concrete as more and more arteries were opened in Manhattan. Long lines of carts and wagons of foodstuff trundled past, and when a milk wagon lumbered by, all the bystanders cheered. She noticed a sign stuck in a snowbank that read: FREE! HELP YOURSELF!

As she neared DiLeo's Bakery, she glimpsed Nick among mounds of snow. His black hair stuck out of his red stocking cap, and he was tossing snow high onto the already towering drift to clear their sidewalk.

For an instant Renée was tempted to cross the street, but she immediately dismissed the idea as nonsense. Didn't she trust herself to be alone with Nick, or was she too embarrassed? Besides, she hadn't seen Nick since the storm and she wanted to know how he'd gotten along.

Nearing Nick, she said in a spritely manner, "Good-morning."

When he looked up and saw Renée, he stopped shoveling. "Good-morning," he replied just as jauntily. "Where are you off to?"

"The *Gazette*," she replied. "I have an article in this morning's edition."

"Wonderful!" Nick exclaimed, looking handsome in his jacket and green muffler. "I knew you could do it." His bronzed face broke into a broad smile, and she realized he was genuinely pleased. Quite a different reaction from Steven's, she thought.

"You're going to be a star reporter one of these days," Nick said, leaning on his shovel and giving her a lazy grin.

"I'm going to try," she said with a laugh. "And you, Nick? What did you do during the storm?"

He chuckled. "Monday morning we sold everything — even two-day-old bread. In the afternoon we cleaned ovens and scrubbed counters and the floor. On Tuesday I hired a cart and went crosstown to buy flour. Papa's busily baking bread, and as soon as I finish shoveling, I'll go in and help him."

"And will your Second Avenue bakery still open on time?"

"We'll open on time," he said, a determined light in his black eyes. "I'll have to work nights, but I can do it."

"You'll be rich, Nick." She smiled at her old friend.

"I have to do something drastic in order to compete with Steven Morison," he replied jocularly.

Her smile faded. "Don't waste your time on me," she said gently. "I'm committed to Steven."

"Then you're serious," he said, his eyes never leaving her face.

"Yes," she answered. "I'm serious. Forget about me, Nick."

"I'll never forget about you," he answered soberly. Then he smiled briefly. "But Papa seems to have given up on you."

"He has?" she asked. She liked Nick's father and was surprised to hear that he no longer considered her for Nick.

Nick threw back his head and laughed. "He's invited the Orsinis and their daughter, Theresa, over for dinner tonight. Mr. Orsini owns several dairy farms in New Jersey. Papa thinks the Orsini cream and butter would be a happy combination with the DiLeo flour and sugar."

"That does sound like a good merger," she said lightly, but her throat was tight. "If Theresa Orsini is as pretty as her name, you'll agree with your father's idea."

"I doubt if she'll measure up to you, Renée," he said, amusement crinkling the corners of his dark eyes.

Renée managed a smile. "I must run."

"I intend to buy six copies of the paper with your story, Renée, and show it to everyone in the neighborhood!"

"You're sweet, Nick," she said softly, walking on.

Jumbled thoughts raced through her mind. So Sam DiLeo was plotting Nick's future already. And

Nick was such an easygoing fellow that she wouldn't be surprised if he'd marry Theresa just to please his father. Oh, Nick, she thought miserably, the girl who gets you will be so lucky.

As she opened the door to the *Gazette*, she wondered why her heart should pound so furiously at the thought of Nick getting married.

Chapter Twenty

WHEN Renée entered the newsroom, newspapers from all over the city were stacked on the table. Hurriedly, she grabbed the *Gazette*, eager to see her story. And there it was! Right on the front page! She avidly scanned her article and was elated that Mr. Webb hadn't deleted one word. Under her headline, "Blizzard Paralyzes City," was her byline — Renée Conti. She was thrilled. After reading it twice, she glanced at the other special editions on the storm. The *World*, the *Sun*, the *Times*, and the *Herald* all carried headlines about the blizzard.

The *Tribune* said, "If Monday will go down as the Day of the Snowflake, Tuesday shall be celebrated as the Day of the Shovel."

Renée read about fifty inches of snow falling in

the New England states, and she was stunned.

"Reading our competition's stories?" Mr. Webb inquired, coming up behind her.

"All the news on the blizzard," she replied, turning around and facing him. "Thank you, Mr. Webb, for leaving my story intact and putting a border around it to make it more prominent."

"I told you it was good," he said with a scowl, but his eyes narrowed to a slight twinkle. "I meant it, too. The *Times* sent a snooper over to find out who Renée Conti is."

"They did?" she asked incredulously.

"I told 'em you were a high school kid and had a full-time job here starting in June."

"I love my work here," she said, her eyes sparkling. "You don't know how exciting it is."

"Well, don't expect a blizzard to come along every time news is slow." His expression held a trace of amused mockery.

"Oh, I won't," she answered, "but other events will happen to write a story about."

"Hmmmph," he said with a shrug and turned to Fred Bromley, who had come up beside him. The tall, thin reporter stared at Renée, giving her an imperceptible nod.

So, Renée thought, this was the dour man she'd be working with in June. She hoped he wouldn't be as gruff as Mr. Webb. Two Mr. Webbs would be hard to take.

Mr. Webb motioned Fred Bromley into his office,

and Renée picked up a second newspaper. She read a list of names that were given to babies born during the storm: Snowflake, Snowdrift, Snowdrop, Storm, Tempest, Gale, and Blizzard. What awful names to saddle a child with for a lifetime, she thought. But certainly babies born on Monday would have March 12, 1888, indelibly marked on their calendar as not only their birthdays, but as the day the worst storm ever to hit New York City occurred.

After she'd sifted through the main stories of the other newspapers, she went into Miss Blossom's office to help her with the footwear layout. Perfect timing, she mused. When the thaw set in, women would be clamoring for boots.

Zena Morison entered, glancing at the display. "Good morning, Renée. I read your story on the blizzard. Congratulations!"

"If it weren't for you, I wouldn't have had such a chance," Renée said. "Even Mr. Webb was pleased," she paused, grinning impishly, "although his smile was more like a grimace."

"That's Mike for you!" Zena said breezily, removing her hat, which was tilted over one eye. "I got caught in a mob of women filling their coal pails," she explained. "Coal has gone from ten cents a pail to a dollar! Disgraceful!" She pursed her lips. "When the store owner announced he was out, several women burst into tears." She shook her head sadly. "I felt so sorry for them. Believe me, our readers are going to hear about the plight of the cold and the hungry!" She shed her coat and prepared to leave, but she turned back. "Oh, I almost forgot. Megan wants to take you to lunch. Can you meet her at The Iron Skillet at noon?"

"I'd love to," Renée exclaimed. "But she doesn't need to do that."

"My daughter insists — she says it's a small price to pay for her life," Zena said dryly, smoothing back a few wisps of her crimson hair. "And I agree."

Renée laughed. "I'll be there at twelve."

"Oh, and another thing," Zena said, pulling a letter out of her pocket. "I had an interesting interview with Mark Twain yesterday. He was writing a letter to his wife and gave me an excerpt. I think it's a good picture of what people were doing who were stuck in hotels. What do you think?"

Renée took the paper and read silently:

> *Blast that blasted dinner party at Dana's! But for that, I — ah! Well, I'm tired, tired calling myself names. Why, I could have been at home all this time. Whereas, here I have been Crusoing on a desert hotel — out of wife, out of children, out of line, and out of cigars, out of every blamed thing in the world that I've any use for. Great Scott!*

Renée chuckled. "His letter makes good copy."

"I wonder how many more, like Mr. Twain, sat

out the storm in a hotel. Thousands, I imagine," Zena said. "Desk clerks were even renting lobby chairs so people could sit up all night."

"At least the storm was good for hotel business," Renée said.

Zena nodded. "But not for shops. Unless, of course, the owners were selling boots or snow shovels. Most stores should have stayed closed. I heard B. Altman's sold only one spool of thread all day." She turned to leave. "I must get to my office."

As Zena left, Miss Blossom bustled in, ready to begin work.

They had only begun the mock-up when Mr. Webb poked his head in Flora's office. "Renée," he said, "forget about the boot display. Fred Bromley needs some help with a paste-up on his story."

Miss Blossom's plump face creased in a smile. "Run along, dear. This display will finish itself."

Renée was thrilled to be asked to work with Mr. Bromley. She'd only said hello to the long-faced, morose man with the heavy pouches under his eyes, but now she had a chance to get to know him. Despite his somber appearance, Mr. Bromley glanced up from his clacking typewriter and nodded civilly.

"Read this copy," he said, throwing a few pages at her. "Mark any mistakes you find." He went back to his typing. "I'll see if I agree."

"Yes, Mr. Bromley," she said, sitting down and immediately reading his story, "The Sea's Killer Wind."

Monday's wicked blizard didn't just paralyze the city, but seamen and ships, as well. The storm, dubbed by seaman as "The Great White Hurricane," took the lives of over one hundred sailors. Of New York's nineteen pilot boats, nine were list and the whole eastern seaboard, from Cape Hatteras to Cape Cod, is strewn with the wreakage of schooners, freighters, sailboats and yachts. It's estimated that over two hundred vessels have fondered at sea, sunk, abandoned or been blown ashore and wrecked.

Renée carefully corrected the simple mistakes Mr. Bromley had made in his typing.

"Well, what do you have?" he asked, noting that she'd put her pencil down.

"Only a few typos," she explained, handing him the copy. "It's a gripping story, Mr. Bromley. I had no idea of all the disasters at sea."

"Yes," he said, stopping to gaze soulfully at her. "So many tragedies. Some men even lashed themselves to the mast to keep from being washed overboard and were later found frozen to death." His soft-spoken words were accompanied by a shake of his head. Returning to his typing, he muttered, "Lunchtime," abruptly dismissing her.

So at twelve o'clock Renée put on her coat, promising Mr. Bromley to be back at one.

Arriving at The Iron Skillet, Renée hurried to a

small table where Megan was already waiting.

"Renée," Megan said, smiling at her. "Come and sit down. I've already ordered for us because I know you have to be back early." She closed the menu and beamed at Renée. "I'm so glad you could come."

"I wouldn't have missed it," Renée answered with a mischievous grin. "It isn't everyday someone buys me lunch."

Megan tilted her head, her blonde hair brushing the fur collar of her dress. Renée suppressed a smile. How different Megan looked from the half-frozen girl she'd dragged out of the snowdrift. She'd never forget the picture of Megan's bedraggled wet hair, her exhausted face, and her blue, stiff lips. Today her curls fell softly around her oval face, and her rust-colored dress gave her porcelain complexion a peachy golden glow.

Megan pulled off her gloves and patted Renée's hand. "I read your story. It's excellent," she said, her eyes wide with surprise. "You know, I think you'll make a good reporter."

"Did you doubt it?" Renée asked teasingly. But she was pleased at Megan's compliment.

For the entire lunch the girls relived Monday's nightmare and were even able to laugh about it.

When they finished dessert, Megan all at once leaned over, touching Renée's hand. "Renée," she said warmly, "you're one of the best friends I've ever had." Her soft brown eyes brimmed with affection. "I've never been able to talk to anyone like I can to you."

Renée almost blurted out, "Not even Alicia?" But when she looked at Megan she knew she meant every word. "I consider you a dear friend, too," she said, pleased that this girl who had everything considered her a friend. For a moment a flash of humor crossed Renée's face, remembering the first time she'd been to dinner at the Morisons and the way Megan had tricked her into using the wrong fork. Now, however, she knew Megan would never do anything to hurt her again. Megan had changed.

"Oh, Renée," Megan said, squeezing her hand. "I'd give anything to have you for a sister-in-law."

Renée stared at her, too astonished to speak. What happened to Megan's concern about social class? Finally, she said with a short laugh, "But Steven and I aren't even engaged."

"I'll have to speak to my brother about that," Megan said promptly, her eyes glinting with amusement. "Renée," she said, "we'd have such fun. We'd be as close as real sisters. Think of all the good times we could share."

"We do have good times," Renée agreed, but suddenly doubts assailed her about cementing a close friendship with Megan. Would they be friends even if she didn't marry Steven? Or would they lose contact? Before, she'd felt Steven's family, especially Megan, was an obstacle to their marriage and this had kept her from becoming too involved. But now she knew Megan truly wanted her to be part of the Morison family. Now she was free to marry Steven. But was he the one for her? Perhaps the family wealth and social position was only an excuse not to rush into an engagement. All at once she was no longer certain. "Megan," she said with a chuckle, pushing aside her muddled thoughts, "things won't be the same. You'll soon be a married lady."

"So?" Megan asked. "What difference will that make? We'd be inseparable. Once you're married to Steven, you'd quit work and we could go shopping together. You'd become a member of the Women's Guild, and in the summer we'd go boating and picnicking. You'd fit in very well with all our friends."

Renée's brows lifted. She never thought she'd hear Megan utter such words. She stood up, tying her scarf around her head. "Time for me to go," she said, feeling her throat tighten. Megan really did love her. "We'll talk later," she said, her eyes luminous with unshed tears. "Thanks for the lunch, Megan."

Megan rose, too. "And I need to get over to Lord & Taylor for a fitting on my going-away outfit." She leaned over and said in a low voice, "Charles and I are going to Newport for our honeymoon. Don't breathe a word!"

"I won't," Renée said, blowing Megan a kiss as she went out the door.

On the way back to work, Renée slowed her steps to a standstill. Why, she wondered, did both Megan and Steven take it for granted that as soon as she married she'd no longer work?

Chapter
Twenty-one

On Saturday afternoon Renée dressed carefully in her new velvet suit and brushed back her long hair, fastening it with two jet-trimmed combs. She smiled, thinking, I'm right in fashion. These beaded combs are just like the ones in the hair-ornament article.

She examined her image in the full-length mirror. Since her struggle in the blizzard, she seemed to have become more mature. Were her eyes a darker shade of blue? Were her cheekbones more pronounced? Was her nose more finely chiseled? Well, she told herself blissfully, she was growing up. And what's more, that day she was going out with Steven! She twirled around, her flared skirts and petticoats flying. She wanted to look her best for him.

After all, she would be meeting the man who might be her future husband. *Might*, she thought, frowning. Before, she'd been sure that she loved Steven, certain that he was the one. But now she wavered, consumed with an inner turmoil, not wanting to make a rash decision. Life was opening up with all kinds of exciting possibilities, and she knew she wasn't ready to settle down.

Aunt Olivia, standing in the doorway, said in admiration, "You look very pretty in your turquoise velvet suit. Your eyes look as azure-blue as the sky today!"

"Thanks to you and Mother for sewing late last night. I love it!" She closed the last frog-fastener at her throat.

"And where are you and Steven going today?" Aunt Olivia asked with a smile playing about her thin lips and a sparkle in her eyes. "If it's any of my business, that is."

Renée faced her, smiling. "Of course it's your business. I owe my whole future to you, Aunt Olivia. If you hadn't convinced Father that I needed a chance to work, I wouldn't be at the *Gazette* or going out with Steven. I'd be engaged to Nick." Nick, she thought with a pang. Dear Nick. She wondered what he was doing. Was he getting his Second Avenue bakery ready to open? And how had he gotten along with Theresa Orsini?

"I can tell you're happy," Olivia said, folding her arms across her chest and examining Renée's face.

"You exude a radiance that I've never seen before." She walked over and straightened the hem of Renée's skirt. "Ah," she said with a low, husky laugh, "to be sixteen again."

"Sometimes being a teenager can be confusing, though," Renée said thoughtfully. "I had lunch with Megan on Wednesday, and she told me how much she wanted me as a sister-in-law."

"That's good," Olivia said, raising her brows inquiringly. "Isn't that what you want?"

Renée said nothing, only staring into Olivia's warm eyes. Her emotions seesawed up and down. Tears welled up in her eyes.

"Isn't Steven the one you want?" Olivia repeated.

"I-I don't know, Aunt Olivia. I'm so mixed up. I don't know if I should marry Steven or not."

"Do you love him?"

"I don't know that, either," she said, her voice breaking.

"Steven can certainly give you everything, but," Olivia warned, her thin face sober, "you will recognize love when it comes. You will know the man who is the one you want to be with forever." She smiled. "When that happens, *mi amore*, then you won't have any doubts."

"Was that the way it was with you and Rinaldo?" Renée questioned, turning back to the mirror but glancing at Olivia's image.

Olivia smiled and her eyes gleamed. "Oh, my, yes. I loved him so much. I wanted to work in the vineyards with him. But Rinaldo wanted me at home." She smiled sadly. "I wish now I had gotten a job so I could have supported myself. Ah, well," she said lightly, "it's a new world, Renée, and you have a choice between a career and marriage."

"I want both," Renée said quickly, tossing her head defiantly. "Isn't that possible?"

Olivia nodded, chuckling. "With you, Renée, anything's possible."

Renée ran to her aunt, hugging her. "You always make me feel better. I love you, Aunt Olivia."

"You're everything to me — like the daughter I never had."

For a moment they remained locked in each other's arms. Then the doorbell rang.

Giving her aunt a final squeeze, Renée ran to answer it.

Steven stood framed in the doorway, tall and handsome, his blond hair tousled from the wind. "Hello, Renée. Ready to do New York today?"

"And what do you have planned?" she asked.

"You'll see," he said mysteriously, holding her coat for her.

As they went down the steps to the carriage, he said in a low voice, "You look more beautiful every time I see you."

"Steven, you spoil me," she replied, stepping up and into the carriage.

"Who better to spoil than my future wife?" he asked jubilantly.

She gave him a worried sideways glance, wishing he wouldn't take so much for granted. She said nothing, however, and looked out the window at the mounds of snow that the "Army of the Shovelers" had piled up. As they drove down Lexington Avenue, Renée read the signs that were stuck in the drifts:

DO YOU GET MY DRIFT?
IT'S SNOW JOKE!
VALUABLE DIAMOND RING LOST IN DRIFT!
   FINDERS KEEPERS.

And in front of a bank, some joker had stuck this sign in a snowbank:

THIS BANK CLOSED INDEFINITELY.

Although it was thawing, she thought, it would be a long time before the mountains of snow melted.

Soon they came to the Staten Island Ferry terminal and Steven glanced at her, grabbing her hand. "Ready for a boat ride?"

"Oh, yes," she said eagerly. The sun was out, glittering over the waters of New York Harbor. A few boats listed heavily in the water, and one was flipped on its side. Most of the wrecked ships, however, had been towed ashore.

Standing on the ferryboat's deck, and leaning on the railing, Renée and Steven watched enthralled as they steamed past the Statue of Liberty. What a marvelous sight to see the Lady holding high her torch. The memory of another day two years ago came back to Renée. The Contis and the DiLeos had packed a picnic lunch and joined the throngs of people to hear President Cleveland's dedication speech for the Statue of Liberty on Bedloe's Island. Her mother had cried, repeating proudly, "The French. The French gave this beautiful monument to America." She remembered how the whole family had crowded around Mrs. Conti and how she had wiped away her mother's tears.

When the "Star-Spangled Banner" had been played, Nick had solemnly placed his arm around her. What happened to those wonderful carefree days of friendship with Nick? She knew what had happened. The ugly words "marriage alliance," spoken by her father, had changed her warm feelings toward Nick to feelings of coolness. Yes, even avoidance.

And now, here she was with Steven, contemplating a marriage that she wouldn't even have considered with Nick. Why? Was it because this engagement was her own idea rather than her father's? She missed Nick. Since he had stayed away, she felt a void in her life.

She glanced at Steven, who pointed to the statue. "Isn't the Lady gorgeous? Even if she is green."

"She is gorgeous," she echoed. "Everything today is gorgeous. After that wild wind and snow it's so good to see the sun." Even the rippled water, calm and blue, danced with dappled sunlight. Debris floated by — a broken mast, a torn sail, several water kegs. But other than that, one would never have guessed these tranquil waters had been a raging torrent the Monday before, tearing ships apart and drowning seamen.

"Be right back," Steven said with a wink. He dashed away and soon returned with two ham sandwiches and two sarsaparillas. "Let's eat over here," he said, leading the way to the boat's prow.

They sat together on a bench, contentedly eating their sandwiches. The air was crisp, but the sun warmed them.

"I'll be going back to Harvard in two weeks," Steven said.

"You are?" Renée said, her eyes widening. She knew he'd be returning to college but hadn't expected it to be this soon.

"Mother is running the newspaper and she's urging me to complete my degree. The estate is settled, so there's nothing holding me here." He tilted his head, gazing at Renée solemnly. "Except you, of course!"

Her eyes met his. How handsome he was. Pensively she remembered his first kiss and the way she'd yearned to spend the rest of her life with him. But now a realization coursed through her. She couldn't be Steven's wife if he didn't support her career!

"Before I go," Steven went on, unaware of her tumultuous thoughts, "I want to give you something."

Suddenly she had a terrifying premonition of what was in the little velvet box that he extracted from his coat pocket. If it was a ring, she didn't want to see it. But before she could place her hand over the box, Steven had snapped it open.

There before her eyes was the largest and most dazzling diamond she'd ever seen!

Carefully Steven took the ring and said tenderly, "Hold out your hand, Renée."

As if mesmerized, she offered him her hand, allowing him to slip it on the third finger of her left hand.

"Will you marry me, Renée?"

All at once she was afraid she'd cry. How could she retreat from Steven's warm love? "I'm just not sure, Steven."

He threw back his head and laughed. "Of course you're sure," he said confidently. "How can you doubt our love? It's special."

She glanced at the flashing diamond. Could she be foolish enough to turn down Steven Morison? How could she even think of refusing him? Yet her agonizing doubts persisted.

Chapter
Twenty-two

RENÉE stared at her diamond engagement ring, which flashed and dazzled in the sun. "Steven," she repeated, "the ring is magnificent, but I can't accept it."

"Nonsense," he said, grinning at her. "Of course you can!"

Entreatingly she gazed at him. "I'm not sure," she said in a low voice. The sea breeze blew over her, and the ferryboat gently rocked. "You're going back to Harvard and I'll be working. I want to wait. We need to be sure." When she saw his stricken expression, she hastily added, "at least for now. When you finish your degree, we can see." Reluctantly, she slipped the ring off her finger and handed it to him.

Carefully he replaced it in the velvet box. "I'll keep this until *you're* sure. *I* have no doubts." He studied her face, his emerald-green eyes shadowed by a somber light. Gently he took her hand. "Will you at least wait for me — be my girl?"

Her heart went out to him. "Yes, Steven," she said, her voice husky. "I'll be here."

"I'll take the train back from Boston every weekend," he teased, a wicked grin lighting his face. "I don't want any of those Saturday night boys cutting in on my territory. Especially Nick."

"Steven," she laughed. "Your studies come first. We'll both be busy, and we can go out when you make it into New York."

He tucked the ring box in his vest pocket. "You're a strong-willed girl, Renée," he observed, an ironic twist to his mouth. "If you want to work after we're married, I'll arrange it so you can go into the office one or two days a week."

She lowered her long lashes so he wouldn't see her blazing blue eyes. He still didn't understand! One or two days, indeed!

"Steven," she said quietly, suppressing her anger and shock with an icy calm, "I don't want you to *arrange* anything! I plan to work full-time." As the ferryboat churned nearer the dock, she rose from the bench, turned away from Steven, and walked over to the rail.

Steven hurried after her. "Sorry, darling, sorry. We'll work something out. You'll see."

She glanced at him, and the amused gleam in his eyes incensed her even more. Everything was so easy for Steven Morison. Whatever he wanted he took. What was it he had said about not wanting anyone to infringe on "his territory"? Well, she wasn't his possession, even if he thought she was. "Steven," she explained firmly, "there's nothing to work out! I plan to continue at the *Gazette*, and that's that."

He gave a slight shrug. "We'll see," he murmured, pulling her close and wrapping his arms around her so that they both faced the New York skyline together.

A breeze ruffled her hair, and she breathed in the tangy salt air, feeling her taut muscles relax. Steven wanted only the best for her. Perhaps she was being unreasonable, she thought as she leaned back in his arms.

"That's my girl," he whispered, brushing her cheek with his lips. Gently, he turned her around and their eyes met. He kissed her, and she forgot her previous misgivings. The rest of the day was spent walking in the park, having a lovely dinner at Carlo's, and enjoying the circus performance at Madison Square Garden. She was surprised to learn that their Monday night performance went on as advertised. There were fewer than one hundred people, but P. T. Barnum said he wouldn't disappoint even one customer.

* * *

When Renée arrived home, it was late, and her father was waiting up.

He pulled out his pocket watch. "Twelve-thirty," he muttered. "Did you tell your mother what time you'd be home?"

"No," she said guiltily. "We went to the circus, and it let out late."

"You and Steven are serious, aren't you?"

Wearily she took off her hat and coat, not wanting a serious discussion. Knowing her father cared about her so much, however, she confided, "Steven offered me a ring today, Father, but I didn't accept it. I'm not ready to be engaged to Steven or to anyone else." She didn't want him to think that just because she'd refused Steven she'd now begin to see Nick. She didn't want to give her father any false hopes.

"You're growing up, little one," he said in a low tone, "and facing some difficult decisions, aren't you?" His eyes softened, and he walked over to her, taking her hand. "Just remember, I'm here if you need to talk."

"I know, Father," she said, giving him a kiss on his cheek and enjoying the feel of his soft beard. "Right now, I'm tired." She pulled her hand free. "Good-night, Father."

John Conti's dark eyes appraised his daughter. "Good-night, Renée. Sleep well."

But sleep wouldn't come as Renée lay in bed, staring at the dark ceiling. Eventually, however, she dozed off and began to dream. Suddenly she was in a black tunnel, racing away from a crowd. At the end of the tunnel she glimpsed a slit of light. If only she could reach that light she'd be safe. The chasing people began to yell and shout at her to stop, but she kept on running. She gasped for breath. She turned and saw Mr. Webb, who pounded after her, waving a rolled-up newspaper over his head. Behind him, she recognized Mr. Bromley, Megan, Miss Blossom, Steven, Nick, Sam DiLeo, and her father. They all wanted something from her. What was it? She couldn't understand their muddled voices. All she wanted was freedom. Just as she was about to reach the open air, Steven, in a final burst of energy, caught up with her, dragging her back. Everyone began pushing and shoving her. Everyone had a demand. She was in a terrible dilemma. She groaned as Steven held her in a tight grip. The clamoring voices created a terrible din in her ears. She awakened with a start, drenched with perspiration. Thunder rumbled in the distance, and lightning slashed across the night sky. She got up to close the window against the driving rain.

Standing silently, she watched the rain beat against the windowpane and run down in rivulets. What did her dream mean? She went back to bed, and this time she fell into a deep, dreamless sleep.

* * *

In the next few days, warm temperatures caused water to run in the streets and gush from rainspouts in torrents. One headline read:

SLUSH, SLOP, SPLASH.

At the *Gazette* Mr. Bromley wrote an editorial about the need for an underground subway, stating that Mayor Abram Hewitt had been stumping to get this through the city legislature. If they'd had underground trains, and if telegraph and telephone wires had been underground, New York City wouldn't have been paralyzed.

In a week's time the city was getting back to normal. Newsboys hawked papers, the mail was delivered, the milkman was back on his regular route, fruit and vegetable stands had fresh produce again, the trains ran on schedule, and the ferryboats were back in full operation. Every kind of vehicle was pressed into service to deliver goods, clogging Broadway and side streets. Carts, drays, horsecar trolleys, vans, and wagons trundled down major avenues, snarling traffic, to bring in meat, groceries, and coal.

After school on Monday on her way to the *Gazette*, Renée sidestepped puddles, and on one corner she had to cross the street to avoid a small lake. Sounds of running, gurgling water and the *plink plink* of dripping water filled her ears.

When she went through the double doors, Steven was on his way out. "Miss Blossom doesn't need you," he said lightly, scarcely slowing his stride as he took her elbow and turned her around, propelling her back through the doors. "Come with me! I'm buying you a cup of coffee," he said, grinning at her.

"B-but — "

"And, furthermore, don't argue with the owner of the *Gazette*!"

She hurried alongside him, trying to keep up. "I thought your mother was the owner," she said, her eyes twinkling.

"Ah, but someday she'll turn everything over to me." He laughed, his even teeth enhancing his handsome face. The cleft in his chin gave him a boyish appeal, and there was a spring to his step.

Renée was happy to see that Steven's spirits were buoyant. He didn't seem depressed that she'd not accepted his ring. But she should have known that. Setbacks only made Steven set his square jaw and work harder toward his goal.

When they were seated in the cafe, Renée had a premonition of what he wanted to speak to her about, but she wanted to avert any more talk about the engagement. "Let's not discuss our future," she said softly. "Let's just talk."

A golden brow arched over one eye, but his good humor never left his face. "All right," he agreed. "What shall we talk about?"

"Well," she said, inclining her head, "tell me about Harvard. What's it like?"

"When you come to Boston, you'll see for yourself. This summer I want you and Megan to visit me." He leaned back in his chair, musing over her question. "What's Harvard University like? We'll walk in the pretty surroundings of Cambridge. The buildings are covered with ivy, and flowers are everywhere."

"I'd love to see it," Renée said, eagerness shining from her bright blue eyes. "If I could only go to college, I'd study writing and literature." She paused, her chin resting in her hands. "What do you do besides attend lectures and study?"

"Oh, we swim in the Charles River, and I'm on the rowing team. I've got a great roommate, Jeremiah Paterson. We have Bread and Butter riots. We — "

"Bread and Butter riots?" she interrupted. "What are they?"

Steven chuckled. "A little poem that Jeremiah made up explains better than I could." He recited Jeremiah's doggerel:

Nathan threw a piece of bread,
And hit Abjah on the head.
The wrathful Freshman, in a trice,
Sent back another bigger slice;
Which, being butter'd pretty well,

Made greasy work wher'er it fell.
And thus arose a fearful battle;
The coffee cups and saucers rattle;
The bread bowls fly at woeful rate . . .

Renée's laughter pealed out. "That's a wonderful poem! Now I know college isn't all classes and studying! What happened after the riot?"

"Not much. Four sophomores were suspended, but other than that, we just had to clean up the dining hall."

"You like college, don't you?"

"It's great," he responded with a smile, "but I'm eager to earn my degree and come back to the *Gazette*. Mother wants me to also." Renée thought Steven would be good for the paper. She gave her attention to him, as he told her more college stories.

They talked and laughed about silly things, and Steven kept his promise, keeping their conversation on a light plane. But when they returned to the *Gazette*, he turned serious. "You know, Megan was quite upset when you didn't accept my ring," he said quietly, taking her hand. "She really wants you for a sister-in-law."

Renée glanced at him sideways. "Megan is a love," she said, "but we must decide our own future, don't you think?"

"And we will," he said, giving a low chuckle. "You'll see. I'll give you the summer at the *Gazette*, and then I bet you'll be ready to settle down."

She placed a finger over his lips. "Shhh," she warned. "No more talk about that!" She blew him a kiss and went through the doors.

As she went toward Miss Blossom's office, she thought sorrowfully that Steven didn't have much faith in her career. Although she hated to admit it, she must tell him she couldn't marry him. Steven wasn't the one for her. He was fun and treated her like a princess, but she really didn't have a loving, equitable relationship with him.

Chapter
Twenty-three

RENÉE hadn't seen Steven for over a week, and she knew he was busy winding up affairs and getting ready to return to Harvard.

On Saturday morning she resolutely boarded the trolley to go to the Morisons. She must tell Steven that she wouldn't be waiting for him and that he should return the diamond ring to the jewelers or save it for someone else. She couldn't let him go on believing that she would be waiting.

She lifted the mansion door's ornate lion's-head knocker.

When Megan answered and saw Renée, she flung open the door. "Come in, Renée, come in," she cried. "What a pleasant surprise!"

Feeling as if her breath was cut off, Renée

stepped inside the wide hall. She didn't dare look at Megan. But could Megan guess from her face what she was about to do? "Wh-where's Steven?" she asked in a tremulous voice.

"Upstairs packing," Megan said. All at once she smiled, touching Renée's wrist. "I need to go in for another fitting next week," she said eagerly. "Let's meet for lunch."

"I-I'll see," Renée said in a strained voice, almost choking on her words. She grasped the banister and ran up the curved staircase.

Steven, packing his valise, turned at the sound of footsteps. He held two folded shirts, which he tossed on the bed when he saw her. Smiling, he held out his arms.

"Steven," she said quickly, before her courage deserted her, "I've come to tell you I can't ever be engaged to you or marry you."

Disbelieving, he stared at her, his green eyes widening. "What do you mean, Renée?"

"It won't work," she said miserably. "I'm sorry."

"Nonsense," he said with a short laugh. "You're upset and don't know what you're saying."

Renée said calmly, "I know exactly what I'm saying."

Steven moved to her side, brushing back a tendril of her hair and letting his fingers trail down her cheek. "Renée," he whispered.

"No, please, Steven," she said firmly, retreating from him. "You'll find another girl, someone who can be a full-time wife and mother." She paused, her voice sinking. "I-I can't." She began to waver. Courage, she told herself, courage. "Forget about me, Steven."

"Renée," he said, trying to keep his tone light, "I can never forget you. We'll talk about this tonight," he said, smiling, "over a romantic candlelight dinner. It's my last night. I'm leaving tomorrow, you know."

"I know," she said. "But I won't be able to see you tonight."

He drew in a sharp intake of air, his expression grim. "You're serious, aren't you?" he said in a soft voice.

"Yes," she whispered. "I'm serious." Teardrops trembled on her lashes. "Good-bye, Steven," she cried, whirling about and dashing out the door. She raced down the stairs, past an astonished Megan, and outside.

Gulping in a lungful of fresh air, she swallowed back her tears. She hated to hurt Steven. He loved her. But when she thought of his good looks and popularity, she was reassured that he'd be all right. He'd soon find someone else.

As she left the trolley and neared DiLeo's Bakery, Nick called to her as he lowered an awning. "Been working, Renée? On Saturday?"

"No," she answered truthfully, not elaborating. She took a deep breath, not wanting him to know that she'd broken up with Steven. She couldn't talk about it yet. Not even to Nick, her oldest friend.

He gave the awning rope a final twist and said, "Will you come to the grand opening of DiLeo's Second Avenue Bakery next Saturday? We're opening sooner than planned." He winked at her. "I'll give you a free doughnut."

She had to laugh, despite her depression. "I'll be there, Nick. I'm eager to see it."

In the next week Renée was assailed by sorrowful regrets over Steven and wondered how he had adjusted. Was he sad, or had he shrugged off her good-bye as just a lesson in life? Several nights she had cried herself to sleep, but now she felt a curious release, a sense of her own worth and freedom. She threw herself into her schoolwork and into historical research for Mr. Bromley, who wanted information on New York when it had been New Amsterdam under the Dutch.

Saturday afternoon she went to DiLeo's opening and had to fight her way through hordes of people. Bread was selling for 2¢ a loaf, and doughnuts were 5¢ a dozen. No wonder everyone was shoving and reaching for bargains.

Nick waved at her. "I've saved you a sack of pastries," he called.

"Give me this apple strudel," a customer shouted at Nick.

He shrugged helplessly, smiling at Renée, and rang up the sale.

"Take ten minutes off, Nick," his mother ordered as she packed up cookies. She looked at Renée and winked, giving Nick a push. "Go on."

Nick untied his apron and picked up a bag of bakery goods. "This is for you," he said, handing it to Renée.

She took the sack of pastries, and they threaded their way through the crowd to stand outdoors near the entrance.

Nick leaned against the building. "Whew," he said, wiping his brow. "It's been like this all morning!"

"Business is good. Your bakery is sure to be a success," she said, proud of Nick.

He glanced at her and said gently, "I heard you broke up with Steven Morison."

"You did?" she questioned, amazed.

"Your mother told my mother," he said, laughing.

She laughed with him. It felt good to laugh again. "But I'm through with romance." she said.

Nick's dark eyes met hers, and she felt warm and secure, wanting to confide in him — to talk to someone about the breakup. But that would come later. "How did you like Theresa Orsini?" she asked, teasing laughter in her eyes.

"A nice girl but a head taller than me and too quiet," he grinned. "She's not for me."

Renée grinnned back. "Do you think you'll ever meet the right one?"

"I've met her," he said with a tip of his head as he gazed into her eyes.

Renée glanced away, her face growing pink.

"I know it's over between us, Renée," he said softly, "but for old times' sake, there's something I've been wanting to do for a long time."

"Oh?" she said, her blue eyes sparkling. "And what's that?"

"A good-bye kiss," he said, touching her cheek and leaning down. He pressed his lips to hers.

Several women going into the bakery chortled gleefully and pointed.

His arms tightened around her, and his kiss became longer. She felt the pulse in her throat begin to throb. Her hands went around his neck. Standing in his close embrace, she didn't care how many bystanders stopped to stare.

Finally, she broke away. "Nick," she said shakily. "You've never kissed me like that before." She backed away, feeling her heart thudding against her rib cage. "I've got to go."

"Good-bye, Renée," Nick said softly. Abruptly, he turned and strode away.

For a moment she couldn't move. She could only gaze at Nick's retreating back. She was astonished at the excitement that coursed through her. As she walked home, she rubbed her moist hands against her skirt, a warm smile broadening her face. An inner voice sang Nick's name over and over, and a warm glow stole over her. She loved Nick! The realization shocked her. Could love happen this fast? With a boy she'd known all her life?

When she arrived home, Tony ran to her. "I finished my kite. Will you go with me to West Park to fly it?"

"Wh-what?" she stammered.

"Oh, forget it," Tony said with a shrug. "You've got that dumb look on your face again."

Olivia looked up from her knitting. "You do look like you're in a trance, my dear. Is something wrong?"

"No, no," she said. "Everything is very all right."

"Did you see Nick at the bakery?"

"Yes, oh, yes, Aunt Olivia. He gave me a whole sack of pastries."

Olivia gave Renée a strange look. "Where is it?" she asked.

"I-I forgot it," Renée said in dismay, helplessly throwing out her hands.

"Better run back and get it."

"Yes," Renée said quickly. "That's what I'll do. I'll go back and get it." She spun about and ran out the door. She wanted to fly back to Nick. What was it that Aunt Olivia had said about being in love? You will recognize love when it comes? She had been in love with Nick all this time and hadn't realized it. But now she knew! There wasn't a doubt in her mind. But would Nick still want her? Did he still love her, or was it too late?

When she arrived at the bakery, it was closed, but she knew bakers. Going around to the back, she opened the door.

Nick, who was kneading a huge mound of bread dough, stopped and stared at her. "Well, hello, again. Did you forget something?" he asked as he sprinkled flour from a large container over the dough.

"Yes," she laughed, not wanting to appear too eager to see him. "The pastries you gave me."

"Oh," he said easily. "I saved them for you. They're on the counter." While he pummeled the dough, she stood awkwardly beside him. "Nick," she said, her voice more unsteady than she would have liked, "there's something else, I-I . . ."

He half turned, giving her a lopsided smile. "Well?"

He wasn't making this easy for her, she thought, feeling a blush of deep crimson steal over her face.

He stopped, looking at her questioningly.

She moved close to him, reaching out her hands, but as she did so she upset the vat of flour, spilling it all over her dress. "Oh, oh," she said, choking on the puffs of flour dust that rose in the air.

Nick, looked at her and swung her into his arms. "Renée," he said, laughing. "You're covered with flour."

"And so are you," she said, giggling.

Nick's dark eyes softened as they gazed at one another. She caught her breath.

"Oh, Nick," she said, loving the feeling of his arms around her. "Is it too late for me? I love you."

"Say that again," he said, a grin spreading across his flour-streaked face.

"I love you," she whispered.

He bent down and kissed her. "You don't know how long I've waited to hear those words from you."

The flour-filled room suffocated her, but she managed to say, "Then it's not too late? You still love me?"

"More than ever," he answered, running his hands through her thick, dark hair and leaving long, white streaks of flour in it.

He backed away. "Look at us," he said with a grin. "We look like a couple of snowmen."

"Nick," she said, half-fearful of his response. "I want to continue to work."

"And I want you to," he said. "After your story on the blizzard, you'll be a star reporter!"

"Oh, Nick," she said ecstatically, "You do understand, don't you?"

"I understand and I also know you're beautiful dipped in flour," he joked, touching his finger to her nose and dotting that with flour, too. He pulled her close. In a husky yet tender voice, he said, "You know you've made me very happy." Suddenly he let out a low peal of laughter, adding, "And think how happy we've made our fathers."

"The marriage alliance they planned worked, after all," Renée said lightly, "But our wedding won't be for a year or two, right? I have a lot to do."

"A year," he murmured against her ear. "I can't wait any longer than that."

"A year," she responded, snuggling deeper into his arms. "That's just right. In a year I'll be the *Gazette*'s star reporter *and* Mrs. Nick DiLeo. What a wonderful combination."

Coming next from Sunfire: JENNIE, who survives the Johnstown flood of 1889 with courage and daring and new hope for love.

SUNFIRE®

Read all about the fascinating young women who lived and loved during America's most turbulent times!

☐ 32774-7		**AMANDA** Candice F. Ransom		$2.95
☐ 33064-0		**SUSANNAH** Candice F. Ransom		$2.95
☐ 33156-6		**DANIELLE** Vivian Schurfranz		$2.95
☐ 33241-4	#5	**JOANNA** Jane Claypool Miner		$2.95
☐ 33242-2	#6	**JESSICA** Mary Francis Shura		$2.95
☐ 33239-2	#7	**CAROLINE** Willo Davis Roberts		$2.95
☐ 33688-6	#14	**CASSIE** Vivian Schurfranz		$2.95
☐ 33686-X	#15	**ROXANNE** Jane Claypool Miner		$2.95
☐ 41468-2	#16	**MEGAN** Vivian Schurfranz		$2.75
☐ 41438-0	#17	**SABRINA** Candice F. Ransom		$2.75
☐ 42134-4	#18	**VERONICA** Jane Claypool Miner		$2.75
☐ 40049-5	#19	**NICOLE** Candice F. Ransom		$2.25
☐ 42228-6	#20	**JULIE** Vivian Schurfranz		$2.75
☐ 40394-X	#21	**RACHEL** Vivian Schurfranz		$2.50
☐ 40395-8	#22	**COREY** Jane Claypool Miner		$2.50
☐ 40717-1	#23	**HEATHER** Vivian Schurfranz		$2.50
☐ 40716-3	#24	**GABRIELLE** Mary Francis Shura		$2.50
☐ 41000-8	#25	**MERRIE** Vivian Schurfranz		$2.75
☐ 41012-1	#26	**NORA** Jeffie Ross Gordon		$2.75
☐ 41191-8	#27	**MARGARET** Jane Claypool Miner		$2.75
☐ 41207-8	#28	**JOSIE** Vivian Schurfranz		$2.75
☐ 41416-X	#29	**DIANA** Mary Francis Shura		$2.75
☐ 42043-7	#30	**RENÉE** Vivian Schurfranz (February '89)		$2.75

Scholastic Inc., P.O. Box 7502, 2932 East McCarty Street, Jefferson City, MO 65102

Please send me the books I have checked above. I am enclosing $ _____
(please add $1.00 to cover shipping and handling). Send check or money-order—no cash or C.O.D.'s please.

Name _____

Address _____

City _____ State/Zip _____

Please allow four to six weeks for delivery. Offer good in U.S.A. only. Sorry, mail order not available to residents of Canada. Prices subject to change.

SUN 888

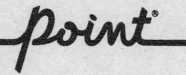

Other books you will enjoy,
about real kids like you!

☐ 42365-7	**Blind Date** R.L. Stine	$2.50
☐ 41248-5	**Double Trouble** Barthe DeClements and Christopher Greimes	$2.75
☐ 41432-1	**Just a Summer Romance** Ann M. Martin	$2.50
☐ 40935-2	**Last Dance** Caroline B. Cooney	$2.50
☐ 41549-2	**The Lifeguard** Richie Tankersley Cusack	$2.50
☐ 33829-3	**Life Without Friends** Ellen Emerson White	$2.75
☐ 40548-9	**A Royal Pain** Ellen Conford	$2.50
☐ 41823-8	**Simon Pure** Julian F. Thompson	$2.75
☐ 40927-1	**Slumber Party** Christopher Pike	$2.50
☐ 41186-1	**Son of Interflux** Gordon Korman	$2.50
☐ 41513-7	**The Tricksters** Margaret Mahy	$2.95
☐ 41546-8	**Yearbook II: Best All-Around Couple** Melissa Davis	$2.50

PREFIX CODE
0-590-

**Available wherever you buy books...
or use the coupon below.**